# Life
## IN THE
# Iron
# Mills
### and Other Stories

THE FEMINIST PRESS
AT THE CITY UNIVERSITY OF NEW YORK
NEW YORK CITY

REBECCA HARDING DAVIS

# Life
## IN THE
# Iron
# Mills
## and Other Stories

EDITED AND WITH A
BIOGRAPHICAL INTERPRETATION
BY TILLIE OLSEN
WITH A NEW FOREWORD BY KIM KELLY

Published in 2020 by the Feminist Press
at the City University of New York
The Graduate Center
365 Fifth Avenue, Suite 5406
New York, NY 10016

feministpress.org

First Feminist Press edition 1972

This book was made possible thanks to a grant from New York State Council on the Arts with the support of Governor Andrew M. Cuomo and the New York State Legislature.

First printing August 2020

Cover and text design by Drew Stevens

**Library of Congress Cataloging-in-Publication Data**
Names: Davis, Rebecca Harding, 1831-1910, author. | Olsen, Tillie, editor.
Title: Life in the iron mills : and other stories / by Rebecca Harding
    Davis ; edited and with a biographical interpretation by Tillie Olsen.
Description: First Feminist Press edition. | New York, NY : The Feminist
    Press, 2020.
Identifiers: LCCN 2020008177 (print) | LCCN 2020008178 (ebook) | ISBN
    9781936932887 (paperback) | ISBN 9781936932894 (ebook)
Subjects: LCSH: Women iron and steel workers--Fiction. | United
    States--Social life and customs--19th century--Fiction.
Classification: LCC PS1517 .A6 2020 (print) | LCC PS1517 (ebook) | DDC
    813/.4--dc23
LC record available at https://lccn.loc.gov/2020008177
LC ebook record available at https://lccn.loc.gov/2020008178

PRINTED IN THE UNITED STATES OF AMERICA

# CONTENTS

# FOREWORD

"A cloudy day; do you know what that is in a town of iron-works?" asks Rebecca Harding Davis in the very first line of her groundbreaking short story "Life in the Iron Mills." Nearly two hundred years after she penned those words, one can still picture how that day must have looked and felt, with the black industrial smoke hanging heavily in the air, ash staining every surface it touches, gray lines carved into the haggard faces of passersby. It must have been hard to breathe, even in younger cities upon whose poisoned earth farmland and forests had once stood. There are places like that now too, cursed with the legacy of humanity's ravenous thirst: vast manufacturing cities in China where everyone wears masks to breathe; polluted air creeping across heavy industry sites in India, Pakistan, and Bangladesh; deforestation fumes choking Cameroon; wildfires in Australia and on the US West Coast, strangling whole towns.

The white-hot wave of industrialization and urbanization that swept the globe in the eighteenth century revolutionized the way that human beings worked, lived, consumed, and died, permanently altered how society functioned, and unwittingly set the stage for the ravages of late capitalism as well as the current climate crisis. Before the Industrial Revolution, agriculture was the primary industry; pollution was minimal, and most people lived in rural areas and worked outdoors. After the great change, laborers flooded into cities in search of work. They found work, all right—but as Davis illustrates, these workers all too often ended up paying a heavy price for it.

In this time, class divisions were redrawn like battle lines, with wealthy capitalists and industrialists indulging their whims for gorgeous mansions while poor- and working-class people were squeezed into rickety boardinghouses, stinking tenements, and dank cellars. When new immigrants came in hopes of building better lives for themselves and their families, they were swept up into the labor pool by greedy bosses who saw a chance to extract as much value from their bodies as possible. It was a miserable time to be alive without the benefit of also being rich. Whether they were native-born or came from elsewhere, a nineteenth-century factory worker's living conditions were utterly grim: diseases ran rampant, sewage pooled in the streets, and people of all ages starved—physically, intellectually, and spiritually. Wage slavery was a death sentence. Some workers paid the cost of urban living with their blood, sweat, and tears, and managed to carve out something resembling a decent existence; others struggled, living hand to mouth, their bodies and spirits broken as soon as they could walk. An unfathomable number paid with their lives.

And for a very long time, their stories were left untold. In a time before public school was both free and compulsory (a feat the United States did not achieve until the 1920s), most members of the laboring class were illiterate, and many immigrant workers were without a firm grasp on the English language. But more importantly—and shamefully—their day-to-day lives were left undocumented and unexamined because almost nobody in the middle and upper classes was listening to what the faceless masses had to say. Those who enjoyed higher social and economic privilege knew that those workers they saw trudging through the streets to and from the mills were doomed to lives that were poor, nasty, brutish, and short, but—then as now—didn't necessarily see it as *their* problem. This is part of what makes "Life in the Iron Mills" and its smoke-smudged take on literary realism so extraordinary. Rebecca Harding Davis was born into a life of relative ease and had next to nothing in common with the workers in her story, and yet she writes about them and the proletarian struggle with such compassion and depth of insight that it's hard to believe she was merely watching from the window.

Davis's story was released more than four decades before another great documentarian of working-class exploitation, Upton Sinclair, ever set foot in a slaughterhouse, and well before the United States had any real labor laws to speak of. When the thirty-year-old Davis sat down to write this story, the Civil War was still in its infancy, the seeds of climate change had been planted but were yet to flower, and the Second Industrial Revolution was still around nine years away. Nine years was also the typical age for a child to be sent to work in the mills. In 1830s Wheeling, West Virginia, where Davis's tale is set, it was common to see children walking by on their way to work in the mornings, their small faces smeared with dirt and drawn thin with malnutrition. Subjecting children to backbreaking labor meant that many died young, and the ones who did survive grew up weak, sickly, and hopeless. And the cycle continued, over and over, as generations of workers were born to suffer and left to die when they lost their usefulness to the factory overlords. As far as the bosses were concerned, labor was abundant and low value. So what if a few little girls lost their arms in the looms, or a couple of little boys were burned to a crisp in the iron works? Humanity was cheap.

In the story, our two main characters, Welsh immigrants Hugh and Deb, were born into a world lit only by fire, their only birthright the same desperate, grinding poverty that had sent their forebears coughing into an early grave. At nineteen, Hugh is already halfway to his own. Men of his time and his profession could only expect to live to thirty-seven if they were lucky, and Hugh was not born a lucky man. Instead, he labors, day after day, night after night, in the heat-blasted belly of the iron works, shoveling pig iron until he can barely lift his scrawny arms. His disabled cousin, Deb, pines after him, but knows he will never love her; she is not beautiful, or clever, or much of anything at all. Her time in the cotton mills has left her body frail and bowed, and any shred of identity that may have blossomed was instead whisked away long ago by the endlessly spinning spools of thread. As much as it hurts, dreaming of Hugh is her only escape from the painful drudgery of her life. But Hugh, a sensitive soul who is mocked by his fellow workers for his shred of education and perceived lack of manliness, is driven by something else—something deep and hungry that threatens to burst from his breast like a wild beast if he tries to ignore its pull. Hugh's dream is to become *someone*, to leave the furnace behind. In lieu of giving away too many details, I will instead leave you with a question posed by a heartless rich man the reader meets later on in the story: "What are taste, reason, to creatures who must live such lives as that?"

What are they, indeed? What are roses to a worker whose only thought is bread? What are dreams to someone who barely has time to sleep? These questions and many others lurk at the heart of this iconic proletarian narrative, daring the reader to chew them over like the slabs of rancid salt pork that Deb wraps up for Hugh's supper. In a time when automation and artificial intelligence have become flash points in the broader conversation around the future of work, it's useful to go back and consider how long that perspective has been percolating in the minds (and theoretical checkbooks) of the corporate oligarchs and petty bourgeoisie, who would ultimately benefit from removing humanity from the entire equation. The pompous mill owner's son, Kirby, says, "If I had the making of men, these men who do the lowest part of the world's work should be machines—nothing more—hands." Now swap in Kirby for a modern-day CEO, and the furnace-tenders for fast-food workers, retail workers, warehouse workers, or autoworkers—current professions that are under threat of being automated away by those who are motivated solely by profits, and see no value in the flesh and blood working the machinery. Everything old is new again, including the tension between the workers who make and the bosses who take. How many more Hughs are out there now, working dangerous, soul-sucking jobs instead of following their passions? How many more will have to suffer before this wretched capitalist system finally breaks down and sets us all free?

Despite its sociopolitical currents, feminist themes, and status as a muckraking classic, "Life in the Iron Mills" is no polemic. Instead, Davis gives her readers an unprecedented glimpse into the souls of working folks at a time when no one else with any platform cared enough to bother. She sifted through the ashes of capitalist carnage to illuminate these workers' rich emotional lives, deep desires, and implacable survival instincts, their solidarity with fellow workers, and their burning hunger for something better. Thanks to her efforts, Hugh and Deb and the millions of real-life workers who lived and died in circumstances just like the ones she set to paper here will live on in proletarian memory as martyrs to the cause of working-class liberation, the unnamed victims of a cruel system that we owe it to them to dismantle.

As Tillie Olsen, who plucked the story out of obscurity in the 1970s and added a biographical sketch of Davis to later expanded versions (like the one you hold in your hands), reminds us, "This was written when almost everywhere the air was pure; and these lives, brought here for the first time into literature, unknown, invisible."

Now, finally, as the world burns around us and the working class has risen up in unprecedented waves, they are invisible no more.

KIM KELLY
February 2020

# LIFE IN THE IRON MILLS
## OR THE KORL WOMAN

You are about to give the life of your reading to a forgotten American classic, Rebecca Harding's *Life in the Iron Mills*, reprinted here after 124 years from the April 1861 *Atlantic Monthly*.

Without precedent or predecessor, it recorded what no one else recorded; alone in its epoch and for decades to come, saw the significance, the presage, in scorned or unseen native materials—and wrought them into art.

Written in secret and in isolation by a thirty-year-old unmarried woman who lived far from literary circles of any kind, it won instant fame—to sleep in ever deepening neglect to our time.

Remember, as you begin to read of the sullen, clinging industrial smoke, the air thick, clammy with the breath of crowded human beings: this was written when almost everywhere the air was pure; and these lives, brought here for the first time into literature, unknown, invisible.

TILLIE OLSEN
1985

*"Is this the end?*
*O Life, as futile, then, as frail!*
*What hope of answer of redress?"*

A cloudy day: do you know what that is in a town of iron-works? The sky sank down before dawn, muddy, flat, immovable. The air is thick, clammy with the breath of crowded human beings. It stifles me. I open the window, and, looking out, can scarcely see through the rain the grocer's shop opposite, where a crowd of drunken Irishmen are puffing Lynchburg tobacco in their pipes. I can detect the scent through all the foul smells ranging loose in the air.

The idiosyncrasy of this town is smoke. It rolls sullenly in slow folds from the great chimneys of the iron-foundries, and settles down in black, slimy pools on the muddy streets. Smoke on the wharves, smoke on the dingy boats, on the yellow river,—clinging in a coating of greasy soot to the house-front, the two faded poplars, the faces of the passers-by. The long train of mules, dragging masses of pig-iron through the narrow street, have a foul vapor hanging to their reeking sides. Here, inside, is a little broken figure of an angel pointing upward from the mantel-shelf; but even its wings are covered with smoke, clotted and black. Smoke everywhere! A dirty canary chirps desolately in a cage beside me. Its dream of green fields and sunshine is a very old dream,—almost worn out, I think.

From the back-window I can see a narrow brick-yard sloping down to the river-side, strewed with rain-butts and tubs. The river, dull and tawny-colored, (*la belle rivière!*) drags itself sluggishly along, tired of the heavy weight of boats and coal-barges. What wonder? When I was a child, I used to fancy a look of weary, dumb appeal upon the face of the negro-like river slavishly bearing its burden day after day. Something of the same idle notion comes to me to-day, when from the street-window I look on the slow stream of human life creeping past, night and morning, to the great mills. Masses of men, with dull, besotted faces bent to the ground, sharpened here and there by pain or cunning; skin and muscle and flesh begrimed with smoke and ashes; stooping all night over boiling cal-drons of metal, laired by day in dens of drunkenness and infamy; breathing from infancy to death an air saturated with fog and grease and soot, vileness for soul and body. What do you make of a case like that, amateur psychologist? You call it an altogether serious thing to be alive: to these men it is a drunken jest, a joke,—horrible to angels perhaps, to them common-place enough. My fancy about the river was an idle one: it is no type of such a life. What if it be stagnant and slimy here? It knows that beyond there waits for it odorous sunlight,—quaint old gardens, dusky with soft, green foliage of apple-trees, and flushing crimson with roses,—air, and fields, and mountains. The future of the Welsh puddler passing just now is not so pleas-ant. To be stowed away, after his grimy work is done, in a hole in the muddy graveyard, and after that,—*not* air, nor green fields, nor curious roses.

Can you see how foggy the day is? As I stand here, idly tapping the windowpane, and looking out through the rain at the dirty back-yard and the coalboats below, fragments of an old story float up before me,—a story of this house into which I happened to come to-day. You may think it a tiresome story enough, as foggy as the day, sharpened by no sudden flashes of pain or pleasure.—I know: only the outline of a dull life, that long since, with thousands of dull lives like its own, was vainly lived and lost: thousands of them, massed, vile, slimy lives, like those of the torpid lizards in yonder stagnant water-butt.—Lost? There is a curious point for you to settle, my friend, who study psychology in a lazy, *dilettante* way. Stop a moment. I am going to be honest. This is what I want you to do. I want you to hide your disgust, take no heed to your clean clothes, and come right down with me,—here, into the thickest of the fog and mud and foul effluvia. I want you to hear this story. There is a secret down here, in this night-mare fog, that has lain dumb for centuries: I want to make it a real thing to you. You, Egoist, or Pantheist, or Arminian, busy in making straight paths for your feet on the hills, do not see it clearly,—this terrible question which men here have gone mad and died trying to answer. I dare not put this secret into words. I told you it was dumb. These men, going by with drunken faces and brains full of unawakened power, do not ask it of Society or of God. Their lives ask it; their deaths ask it. There is no reply. I will tell you plainly that I have a great hope; and I bring it to you to be tested. It is this: that this terrible dumb question is its own reply; that it is not the sentence of death we think it, but, from the very extremity of its darkness, the most solemn prophecy which the world has known of the Hope to come. I dare make my meaning no clearer, but will only tell my story. It will, perhaps, seem to you as foul and dark as this thick vapor about us, and as pregnant with death; but if your eyes are free as mine are to look deeper, no perfume-tinted dawn will be so fair with promise of the day that shall surely come.

My story is very simple,—only what I remember of the life of one of these men,—a furnace-tender in one of Kirby & John's rolling-mills,—Hugh Wolfe. You know the mills? They took the great order for the lower Virginia railroads there last winter; run usually with about a thousand men. I cannot tell why I choose the half-forgotten story of this Wolfe more than that of myriads of these furnace-hands. Perhaps because there is a secret, underlying sympathy between that story and this day with its impure fog and thwarted sunshine,—or perhaps simply for the reason that this house is the one where the Wolfes lived. There were the father and son,—both hands, as I said, in one of Kirby & John's mills for making railroad-iron,—and Deborah, their cousin, a picker in some of the cotton-mills. The house was rented then to half a dozen families. The Wolfes had two of the cellar-rooms. The old man, like many of the puddlers and feeders of the mills, was

Welsh,—had spent half of his life in the Cornish tin-mines. You may pick the Welsh emigrants, Cornish miners, out of the throng passing the windows, any day. They are a trifle more filthy; their muscles are not so brawny; they stoop more. When they are drunk, they neither yell, nor shout, nor stagger, but skulk along like beaten hounds. A pure, unmixed blood, I fancy: shows itself in the slight angular bodies and sharply-cut facial lines. It is nearly thirty years since the Wolfes lived here. Their lives were like those of their class: incessant labor, sleeping in kennel-like rooms, eating rank pork and molasses, drinking—God and the distillers only know what; with an occasional night in jail, to atone for some drunken excess. Is that all of their lives?—of the portion given to them and these their duplicates swarming the streets to-day?—nothing beneath?—all? So many a political reformer will tell you,—and many a private reformer, too, who has gone among them with a heart tender with Christ's charity, and come out out-raged, hardened.

One rainy night, about eleven o'clock, a crowd of half-clothed women stopped outside of the cellar-door. They were going home from the cotton-mill.

"Good-night, Deb," said one, a mulatto, steadying herself against the gas-post. She needed the post to steady her. So did more than one of them.

"Dah's a ball to Miss Potts' to-night. Ye'd best come."

"Inteet, Deb, if hur'll come, hur'll hef fun," said a shrill Welsh voice in the crowd.

Two or three dirty hands were thrust out to catch the gown of the woman, who was groping for the latch of the door.

"No."

"No? Where's Kit Small, then?"

"Begorra! on the spools. Alleys behint, though we helped her, we dud. An wid ye! Let Deb alone! It's ondacent frettin' a quite body. Be the powers, an we'll have a night of it! there'll be lashin's o' drink,—the Vargent be blessed and praised for't!"

They went on, the mulatto inclining for a moment to show fight, and drag the woman Wolfe off with them; but, being pacified, she staggered away.

Deborah groped her way into the cellar, and, after considerable stumbling, kindled a match, and lighted a tallow dip, that sent a yellow glimmer over the room. It was low, damp,—the earthen floor covered with a green, slimy moss,—a fetid air smothering the breath. Old Wolfe lay asleep on a heap of straw, wrapped in a torn horse-blanket. He was a pale, meek little man, with a white face and red rabbit-eyes. The woman Deborah was like him; only her face was even more ghastly, her lips bluer, her eyes more watery. She wore a faded cotton gown and a slouching bonnet. When she walked, one could see that she was deformed, almost a hunchback. She trod softly, so as not to waken him, and went through into the room beyond. There she found by the half-extinguished fire an iron saucepan filled with cold boiled potatoes, which she put upon a broken chair with a pint-cup of ale. Placing the old candlestick beside this dainty repast, she untied her bonnet, which hung limp and wet over her face, and prepared to eat her supper. It was the first food that had touched her lips since morning. There was enough of it, however: there is not always. She was hungry,—one could see that easily enough,—and not drunk, as most of her companions would have been found at this hour. She did not drink, this woman,—her face told that, too,—nothing stronger than ale. Perhaps the weak, flaccid wretch had some stimulant in her pale life to keep her up,—some love or hope, it might be, or urgent need. When that stimulant was gone, she would take to whiskey. Man cannot live by work alone. While she was skinning the potatoes, and munching them, a noise behind her made her stop.

"Janey!" she called, lifting the candle and peering into the darkness. "Janey, are you there?"

A heap of ragged coats was heaved up, and the face of a young girl emerged, staring sleepily at the woman.

"Deborah," she said, at last, "I'm here the night."

"Yes, child. Hur's welcome," she said, quietly eating on.

The girl's face was haggard and sickly; her eyes were heavy with sleep and hunger: real Milesian eyes they were, dark, delicate blue, glooming out from black shadows with a pitiful fright.

"I was alone," she said, timidly.

"Where's the father?" asked Deborah, holding out a potato, which the girl greedily seized.

"He's beyant,—wid Haley,—in the stone house."

(Did you ever hear the word *jail* from an Irish mouth?)
"I came here. Hugh told me never to stay me-lone."

"Hugh?"

"Yes."

A vexed frown crossed her face. The girl saw it, and added quickly,—

"I have not seen Hugh the day, Deb. The old man says his watch lasts till the mornin'."

The woman sprang up, and hastily began to arrange some bread and flitch in a tin pail,* and to pour her own measure of ale into a bottle. Tying on her bonnet, she blew out the candle.

"Lay ye down, Janey dear," she said, gently, covering her with the old rags. "Hur can eat the potatoes, if hur's hungry.

"Where are ye goin', Deb? The rain's sharp."

"To the mill, with Hugh's supper."

"Let him bide till th' morn. Sit ye down."

"No, no,"—sharply pushing her off. "The boy'll starve."

She hurried from the cellar, while the child wearily coiled herself up for sleep. The rain was falling heavily, as the woman, pail in hand, emerged from the mouth of the alley, and turned down the narrow street, that stretched out, long and black, miles before her. Here and there a flicker of gas lighted an uncertain space of muddy footwalk and gutter; the long rows of houses,

---

*The "flitch" which Deb packs with bread into the pail for Wolfe's dinner is rank salt pork.

except an occasional lager-bier shop, were closed; now and then she met a band of mill-hands skulking to or from their work.

Not many even of the inhabitants of a manufacturing town know the vast machinery of system by which the bodies of workmen are governed, that goes on unceasingly from year to year. The hands of each mill are divided into watches that relieve each other as regularly as the sentinels of an army. By night and day the work goes on, the unsleeping engines groan and shriek, the fiery pools of metal boil and surge. Only for a day in the week, in half-courtesy to public censure, the fires are partially veiled; but as soon as the clock strikes midnight, the great furnaces break forth with renewed fury, the clamor begins with fresh, breathless vigor, the engines sob and shriek like "gods in pain."

As Deborah hurried down through the heavy rain, the noise of these thousand engines sounded through the sleep and shadow of the city like far-off thunder. The mill to which she was going lay on the river, a mile below the city-limits. It was far, and she was weak, aching from standing twelve hours at the spools. Yet it was her almost nightly walk to take this man his supper, though at every square she sat down to rest, and she knew she should receive small word of thanks.

Perhaps, if she had possessed an artist's eye, the picturesque oddity of the scene might have made her step stagger less, and the path seem shorter; but to her the mills were only "summat deilish to look at by night."

The road leading to the mills had been quarried from the solid rock, which rose abrupt and bare on one side of the cinder-covered road, while the river, sluggish and black, crept past on the other. The mills for rolling iron are simply immense tent-like roofs, covering acres of ground, open on every side. Beneath these roofs Deborah looked in on a city of fires, that burned hot and fiercely in the night. Fire in every horrible form: pits of flame waving in the wind; liquid metal-flames writhing in tortuous streams through the sand; wide caldrons filled with boiling fire, over which bent ghastly wretches stirring the strange brewing; and through all, crowds of half-clad men, looking like revengeful ghosts in the red light, hurried, throwing masses of glittering fire. It was like a street in Hell. Even Deborah muttered, as she crept through, "looks like t' Devil's place!" It did,—in more ways than one.

She found the man she was looking for, at last, heaping coal on a furnace. He had not time to eat his supper; so she went behind the furnace, and waited. Only a few men were with him, and they noticed her only by a "Hyur comes t'hunchback, Wolfe."

Deborah was stupid with sleep; her back pained her sharply; and her teeth chattered with cold, with the rain that soaked her clothes and dripped from her at every step. She stood, however, patiently holding the pail, and waiting.

"Hout, woman! ye look like a drowned cat. Come near to the fire,"—said one of the men, approaching to scrape away the ashes.

She shook her head. Wolfe had forgotten her. He turned, hearing the man, and came closer.

"I did no' think; gi' me my supper, woman."

She watched him eat with a painful eagerness. With a woman's quick instinct, she saw that he was not hungry,—was eating to please her. Her pale, watery eyes began to gather a strange light.

"Is't good, Hugh? T' ale was a bit sour, I feared."

"No, good enough." He hesitated a moment. "Ye're tired, poor lass! Bide here till I go. Lay down there on that heap of ash, and go to sleep."

He threw her an old coat for a pillow, and turned to his work. The heap was the refuse of the burnt iron, and was not a hard bed; the half-smothered warmth, too, penetrated her limbs, dulling their pain and cold shiver.

Miserable enough she looked, lying there on the ashes like a limp, dirty rag,—yet not an unfitting figure to crown the scene of hopeless discomfort and veiled crime: more fitting, if one looked deeper into the heart of things, at her thwarted woman's form, her colorless life, her waking stupor that smothered pain and hunger,—even more fit to be a type of her class. Deeper yet if one could look, was there nothing worth reading in this wet, faded thing, half-covered with ashes? no story of a soul filled with groping passionate love, heroic unselfishness, fierce jealousy? of years of weary trying to please the one human being whom she loved, to gain one look of real heart-kindness from him? If anything like this were hidden beneath the pale, bleared eyes, and dull, washed-out-looking face, no one had ever taken the trouble to read its faint signs: not the half-clothed furnace-tender, Wolfe, certainly. Yet he was kind to her: it was his nature to be kind, even to the very rats that swarmed in the cellar: kind to her in just the same way. She knew that. And it might be that very knowledge had given to her face its apathy and vacancy more than her low, torpid life. One sees that dead, vacant look steal sometimes over the rarest, finest of women's faces,—in the very midst, it may be, of their warmest summer's day; and then one can guess at the secret of intolerable solitude that lies hid beneath the delicate laces and brilliant smile. There was no warmth, no brilliancy, no summer for this woman; so the stupor and vacancy had time to gnaw into her face perpetually. She was young, too, though no one guessed it; so the gnawing was the fiercer.

She lay quiet in the dark corner, listening, through the monotonous din and uncertain glare of the works, to the dull plash of the rain in the far distance,—shrinking back whenever the man Wolfe happened to look towards her. She knew, in spite of all his kindness, that there was that in her face and form which made him loathe the sight of her. She felt by instinct, although she could not comprehend it, the finer nature of the man, which made him among his fellow-workmen something unique, set apart. She knew, that, down under all the vileness and coarseness of his life, there was a groping passion for whatever was beautiful and pure,— that his soul sickened with disgust at her deformity, even when his words were kindest. Through this dull consciousness, which never left her, came, like a sting, the recollection of the dark blue eyes and lithe figure of the little Irish girl she had left in the cellar. The recollection struck through even her stupid intellect with a vivid glow of beauty and of grace. Little Janey, timid, helpless, clinging to Hugh as her only friend: that was the sharp thought, the bitter thought, that drove into the glazed eyes a fierce light of pain. You laugh at it? Are pain and jealousy less savage realities down here in this place I am taking you to than in your own house or your own heart,—your heart, which they clutch at sometimes? The note is the same, I fancy, be the octave high or low.

If you could go into this mill where Deborah lay, and drag out from the hearts of these men the terrible tragedy of their lives, taking it as a symptom of the disease of their class, no ghost Horror would terrify you more. A reality of soul-starvation, of living death, that meets you every day under the besotted faces on the street,—I can paint nothing of this, only give you the outside outlines of a night, a crisis in the life of one man: whatever muddy depth of soul-history lies beneath you can read according to the eyes God has given you.

Wolfe, while Deborah watched him as a spaniel its master, bent over the furnace with his iron pole, unconscious of her scrutiny, only stopping to receive orders. Physically, Nature had promised the man but little. He had already lost the strength and instinct vigor of a man, his muscles were thin, his nerves weak, his face (a meek, woman's face) haggard, yellow with consumption. In the mill he was known as one of the girl-men: "Molly Wolfe" was his *sobriquet*. He was never seen in the cockpit, did not own a terrier, drank but seldom; when he did, desperately. He fought sometimes, but was always thrashed, pommelled to a jelly. The man was game enough, when his blood was up: but he was no favorite in the mill; he had the taint of school-learning on him,—not to a dangerous extent, only a quarter or so in the free-school in fact,* but enough to ruin him as a good hand in a fight.

For other reasons, too, he was not popular. Not one of themselves, they felt that, though outwardly as filthy and ash-covered; silent, with foreign thoughts and longings breaking out through his quietness in innumerable curious ways: this one, for instance. In the neighboring furnace-buildings lay great heaps of the refuse from the ore after the pig-metal is run. *Korl* we call it here: a light, porous substance, of a delicate, waxen, flesh-colored tinge. Out of the blocks of this korl, Wolfe, in his off-hours from the furnace, had a habit of chipping and moulding figures,—hideous, fantastic enough, but sometimes strangely beautiful: even the mill-men saw that, while they jeered at him. It was a curious fancy in the man, almost a passion. The few hours for rest he spent hewing and hacking with his blunt knife, never speaking, until his watch came again,—working at one figure for months, and, when it was finished, breaking it to pieces perhaps, in a fit

---

*Most workers in the mills were illiterate, public schools almost nonexistent.

of disappointment. A morbid, gloomy man, untaught, unled, left to feed his soul in grossness and crime, and hard, grinding labor.

I want you to come down and look at this Wolfe, standing there among the lowest of his kind, and see him just as he is, that you may judge him justly when you hear the story of this night. I want you to look back, as he does every day, at his birth in vice, his starved infancy; to remember the heavy years he has groped through as boy and man,—the slow, heavy years of constant, hot work. So long ago he began, that he thinks sometimes he has worked there for ages. There is no hope that it will ever end. Think that God put into this man's soul a fierce thirst for beauty,—to know it, to create it; to *be*—something, he knows not what,—other than he is. There are moments when a passing cloud, the sun glinting on the purple thistles, a kindly smile, a child's face, will rouse him to a passion of pain,— when his nature starts up with a mad cry of rage against God, man, whoever it is that has forced this vile, slimy life upon him. With all this groping, this mad desire, a great blind intellect stumbling through wrong, a loving poet's heart, the man was by habit only a coarse, vulgar laborer, familiar with sights and words you would blush to name. Be just: when I tell you about this night, see him as he is. Be just,—not like man's law, which seizes on one isolated fact, but like God's judging angel, whose clear, sad eye saw all the countless cankering days of this man's life, all the countless nights, when, sick with starving, his soul fainted in him, before it judged him for this night, the saddest of all.

I called this night the crisis of his life. If it was, it stole on him unawares. These great turning-days of life cast no shadow before, slip by unconsciously. Only a trifle, a little turn of the rudder, and the ship goes to heaven or hell.

Wolfe, while Deborah watched him, dug into the furnace of melting iron with his pole, dully thinking only how many rails the lump would yield. It was late,— nearly Sunday morning; another hour, and the heavy work would be done, only the furnaces to replenish and cover for the next day. The workmen were growing more noisy, shouting, as they had to do, to be heard over the deep clamor of the mills. Suddenly they grew less boisterous,—at the far end, entirely silent. Something unusual had happened. After a moment, the silence came nearer; the men stopped their jeers and drunken choruses. Deborah, stupidly lifting up her head, saw the cause of the quiet. A group of five or six men were slowly approaching, stopping to examine each furnace as they came. Visitors often came to see the mills after night: except by growing less noisy, the men took no notice of them. The furnace where Wolfe worked was near the bounds of the works; they halted there hot and tired: a walk over one of these great foundries is no trifling task. The woman, drawing out of sight, turned over to sleep. Wolfe, seeing them stop, suddenly roused from his indifferent stupor, and watched them keenly. He knew some of them: the overseer, Clarke,—a son of Kirby, one of the mill-owners,—and a Doctor May, one of the town-physicians. The other two were strangers.

Wolfe came closer. He seized eagerly every chance that brought him into contact with this mysterious class that shone down on him perpetually with the glamour of another order of being. What made the difference between them? That was the mystery of his life. He had a vague notion that perhaps to-night he could find it out. One of the strangers sat down on a pile of bricks, and beckoned young Kirby to his side.

"This *is* hot, with a vengeance. A match, please?"— lighting his cigar. "But the walk is worth the trouble. If it were not that you must have heard it so often, Kirby, I would tell you that your works look like Dante's Inferno."

Kirby laughed.

"Yes. Yonder is Farinata himself in the burning tomb,"—pointing to some figure in the shimmering shadows.

"Judging from some of the faces of your men," said the other, "they bid fair to try the reality of Dante's vision, some day."

Young Kirby looked curiously around, as if seeing the faces of his hands for the first time.

"They're bad enough, that's true. A desperate set, I fancy. Eh, Clarke?"

The overseer did not hear him. He was talking of net profits just then,—giving, in fact, a schedule of the annual business of the firm to a sharp peering little Yankee, who jotted down notes on a paper laid on the crown of his hat: a reporter for one of the city-papers, getting up a series of reviews of the leading manufactories. The other gentlemen had accompanied them merely for amusement. They were silent until the notes were finished, drying their feet at the furnaces, and sheltering their faces from the intolerable heat. At last the overseer concluded with—

"I believe that is a pretty fair estimate, Captain."

"Here, some of you men!" said Kirby, "bring up those boards. We may as well sit down, gentlemen, until the rain is over. It cannot last much longer at this rate."

"Pig-metal,"—mumbled the reporter,—"um! coal facilities,—um! hands employed, twelve hundred,—bitumen,—um!—all right, I believe, Mr. Clarke;—sinking-fund,—what did you say was your sinking-fund?"

"Twelve hundred hands?" said the stranger, the young man who had first spoken. "Do you control their votes, Kirby?"

"Control? No." The young man smiled complacently. "But my father brought seven hundred votes to the polls for his candidate last November. No force-work, you understand,—only a speech or two, a hint to form themselves into a society, and a bit of red and blue bunting to make them a flag. The Invincible Roughs,—I believe that is their name. I forget the motto: 'Our country's hope,' I think."

There was a laugh. The young man talking to Kirby sat with an amused light in his cool gray eye, surveying critically the half-clothed figures of the puddlers, and the slow swing of their brawny muscles. He was a stranger in the city,—spending a couple of months in the borders of a Slave State, to study the institutions of the South,—a brother-in-law of Kirby's,—Mitchell. He was an amateur gymnast,—hence his anatomical eye; a patron, in a *blasé* way, of the prize-ring; a man who sucked the essence out of a science or philosophy in an indifferent, gentlemanly way; who took Kant, Novalis, Humboldt, for what they were worth in his own scales; accepting all, despising nothing, in heaven, earth, or hell, but one-idead men; with a temper yielding and brilliant as summer water, until his Self was touched, when it was ice, though brilliant still. Such men are not rare in the States.

As he knocked the ashes from his cigar, Wolfe caught with a quick pleasure the contour of the white hand, the blood-glow of a red ring he wore. His voice, too, and that of Kirby's, touched him like music,—low, even, with chording cadences. About this man Mitchell hung the impalpable atmosphere belonging to the thoroughbred gentleman. Wolfe, scraping away the ashes beside him, was conscious of it, did obeisance to it with his artist sense, unconscious that he did so.

The rain did not cease. Clarke and the reporter left the mills; the others, comfortably seated near the furnace, lingered, smoking and talking in a desultory way. Greek would not have been more unintelligible to the furnace-tenders, whose presence they soon forgot entirely. Kirby drew out a newspaper from his pocket and read aloud some article, which they discussed eagerly. At every sentence, Wolfe listened more and more like a dumb, hopeless animal, with a duller, more stolid look creeping over his face, glancing now and then at Mitchell, marking acutely every smallest sign of refinement, then back to himself, seeing as in a mirror his filthy body, his more stained soul.

Never! He had no words for such a thought, but he knew now, in all the sharpness of the bitter certainty, that between them there was a great gulf never to be passed. Never!

The bell of the mills rang for midnight. Sunday morning had dawned. Whatever hidden message lay in the tolling bells floated past these men unknown. Yet it was there. Veiled in the solemn music ushering the risen Saviour was a key-note to solve the darkest secrets of a world gone wrong,—even this social riddle which the brain of the grimy puddler grappled with madly to-night.

The men began to withdraw the metal from the caldrons. The mills were deserted on Sundays, except by the hands who fed the fires, and those who had no lodgings and slept usually on the ash-heaps. The three strangers sat still during the next hour, watching the men cover the furnaces, laughing now and then at some jest of Kirby's.

"Do you know," said Mitchell, "I like this view of the works better than when the glare was fiercest? These heavy shadows and the amphitheatre of smothered fires are ghostly, unreal. One could fancy these red smouldering lights to be the half-shut eyes of wild beasts, and the spectral figures their victims in the den."

Kirby laughed. "You are fanciful. Come, let us get out of the den. The spectral figures, as you call them, are a little too real for me to fancy a close proximity in the darkness,—unarmed, too."

The others rose, buttoning their overcoats, and lighting cigars.

"Raining, still," said Doctor May, "and hard. Where did we leave the coach, Mitchell?"

"At the other side of the works.—Kirby, what's that?"

Mitchell started back, half-frightened, as, suddenly turning a corner, the white figure of a woman faced him in the darkness,—a woman, white, of giant proportions, crouching on the ground, her arms flung out in some wild gesture of warning.

"Stop! Make that fire burn there!" cried Kirby, stopping short.

The flame burst out, flashing the gaunt figure into bold relief.

Mitchell drew a long breath.

"I thought it was alive," he said, going up curiously.

The others followed.

"Not marble, eh?" asked Kirby, touching it.

One of the lower overseers stopped.

"Korl, Sir."

"Who did it?"

"Can't say. Some of the hands; chipped it out in off-hours."

"Chipped to some purpose, I should say. What a flesh-tint the stuff has! Do you see, Mitchell?"

"I see."

He had stepped aside where the light fell boldest on the figure, looking at it in silence. There was not one line of beauty or grace in it: a nude woman's form, muscular, grown coarse with labor, the powerful limbs instinct with some one poignant longing. One idea: there it was in the tense, rigid muscles, the clutching hands, the wild, eager face, like that of a starving wolf's. Kirby and Doctor May walked around it, critical, curious. Mitchell stood aloof, silent. The figure touched him strangely.

"Not badly done," said Doctor May, "Where did the fellow learn that sweep of the muscles in the arm and hand? Look at them! They are groping, do you see?—clutching: the peculiar action of a man dying of thirst."

"They have ample facilities for studying anatomy," sneered Kirby, glancing at the half-naked figures.

"Look," continued the Doctor, "at this bony wrist, and the strained sinews of the instep! A working-woman,—the very type of her class."

"God forbid!" muttered Mitchell.

"Why?" demanded May, "What does the fellow intend by the figure? I cannot catch the meaning."

"Ask him," said the other, dryly, "There he stands,"—pointing to Wolfe, who stood with a group of men, leaning on his ash-rake.

The Doctor beckoned him with the affable smile which kind-hearted men put on, when talking to these people.

"Mr. Mitchell has picked you out as the man who did this,—I'm sure I don't know why. But what did you mean by it?"

"She be hungry."

Wolfe's eyes answered Mitchell, not the Doctor.

"Oh-h! But what a mistake you have made, my fine fellow! You have given no sign of starvation to the body. It is strong,—terribly strong. It has the mad, half-despairing gesture of drowning."

Wolfe stammered, glanced appealingly at Mitchell, who saw the soul of the thing, he knew. But the cool, probing eyes were turned on himself now,—mocking, cruel, relentless.

"Not hungry for meat," the furnace-tender said at last.

"What then? Whiskey?" jeered Kirby, with a coarse laugh.

Wolfe was silent a moment, thinking.

"I dunno," he said, with a bewildered look. "It mebbe. Summat to make her live, I think,—like you. Whiskey ull do it, in a way."

The young man laughed again. Mitchell flashed a look of disgust somewhere,—not at Wolfe.

"May," he broke out impatiently, "are you blind? Look at that woman's face! It asks questions of God, and says, 'I have a right to know,' Good God, how hungry it is!"

They looked a moment; then May turned to the mill-owner:—

"Have you many such hands as this? What are you going to do with them? Keep them at puddling iron?"

Kirby shrugged his shoulders. Mitchell's look had irritated him.

"*Ce n'est pas mon affaire.* I have no fancy for nursing

infant geniuses. I suppose there are some stray gleams of mind and soul among these wretches. The Lord will take care of his own; or else they can work out their own salvation. I have heard you call our American system a ladder which any man can scale. Do you doubt it? Or perhaps you want to banish all social ladders, and put us all on a flat table-land,—eh, May?"

The Doctor looked vexed, puzzled. Some terrible problem lay hid in this woman's face, and troubled these men. Kirby waited for an answer, and, receiving none, went on, warming with his subject.

"I tell you, there's something wrong that no talk of '*Liberté*' or '*Egalité*' will do away. If I had the making of men, these men who do the lowest part of the world's work should be machines,—nothing more,—hands. It would be kindness. God help them! What are taste, reason, to creatures who must live such lives as that?" He pointed to Deborah, sleeping on the ash-heap. "So many nerves to sting them to pain. What if God had put your brain, with all its agony of touch, into your fingers, and bid you work and strike with that?"

"You think you could govern the world better?" laughed the Doctor.

"I do not think at all."

"That is true philosophy. Drift with the stream, because you cannot dive deep enough to find bottom, eh?"

"Exactly," rejoined Kirby. "I do not think. I wash my hands of all social problems,—slavery, caste, white or black. My duty to my operatives has a narrow limit,—

the pay-hour on Saturday night. Outside of that, if they cut korl, or cut each other's throats, (the more popular amusement of the two,) I am not responsible."

The Doctor sighed,—a good honest sigh, from the depths of his stomach.

"God help us! Who is responsible?"

"Not I, I tell you," said Kirby, testily. "What has the man who pays them money to do with their souls' concerns, more than the grocer or butcher who takes it?"

"And yet," said Mitchell's cynical voice, "look at her! How hungry she is!"

Kirby tapped his boot with his cane. No one spoke. Only the dumb face of the rough image looking into their faces with the awful question, "What shall we do to be saved?" Only Wolfe's face, with its heavy weight of brain, its weak, uncertain mouth, its desperate eyes, out of which looked the soul of his class,—only Wolfe's face turned towards Kirby's. Mitchell laughed,—a cool, musical laugh.

"Money has spoken!" he said, seating himself lightly on a stone with the air of an amused spectator at a play. "Are you answered?"—turning to Wolfe his clear, magnetic face.

Bright and deep and cold as Arctic air, the soul of the man lay tranquil beneath. He looked at the furnace-tender as he had looked at a rare mosaic in the morning; only the man was the more amusing study of the two.

"Are you answered? Why, May, look at him! *'De profundis clamavi.'* Or, to quote in English, 'Hungry and thirsty, his soul faints in him.' And so Money sends back its answer into the depths through you, Kirby! Very clear the answer, too!—I think I remember reading the same words somewhere: washing your hands in Eau de Cologne, and saying, 'I am innocent of the blood of this man. See ye to it!'"

Kirby flushed angrily.

"You quote Scripture freely."

"Do I not quote correctly? I think I remember another line, which may amend my meaning? 'Inasmuch as ye did it unto one of the least of these, ye did it unto me.' Deist? Bless you, man, I was raised on the milk of the Word. Now, Doctor, the pocket of the world having uttered its voice, what has the heart to say? You are a philanthropist, in a small Way,—*n'est ce pas?* Here, boy, this gentleman can show you how to cut korl better,—or your destiny. Go on, May!"

"I think a mocking devil possesses you to-night," rejoined the Doctor, seriously.

He went to Wolfe and put his hand kindly on his arm. Something of a vague idea possessed the Doctor's brain that much good was to be done here by a friendly word or two: a latent genius to be warmed into life by a waited-for sunbeam. Here it was: he had brought it. So he went on complacently:—

"Do you know, boy, you have it in you to be a great sculptor, a great man?—do you understand?" (talking down to the capacity of his hearer: it is a way people have with children, and men like Wolfe,)—"to live a better, stronger life than I, or Mr. Kirby here? A man may make himself anything he chooses. God has given you stronger powers than many men,—me, for instance."

May stopped, heated, glowing with his own magnanimity. And it was magnanimous. The puddler had drunk in every word, looking through the Doctor's flurry, and generous heat, and self-approval, into his will, with those slow, absorbing eyes of his.

"Make yourself what you will. It is your right."

"I know," quietly. "Will you help me?"

Mitchell laughed again. The Doctor turned now, in a passion,—

"You know, Mitchell, I have not the means. You know, if I had, it is in my heart to take this boy and educate him for"—

"The glory of God, and the glory of John May."

May did not speak for a moment; then, controlled, he said,—

"Why should one be raised, when myriads are left?—I have not the money, boy," to Wolfe, shortly.

"Money?" He said it over slowly, as one repeats the guessed answer to a riddle, doubtfully. "That is it? Money?"

"Yes, money,—that is it," said Mitchell, rising, and drawing his furred coat about him. "You've found the cure for all the world's diseases.—Come, May, find your good-humor, and come home. This damp wind chills my very bones. Come and preach your Saint-Simonian doctrines' to-morrow to Kirby's hands. Let them have a clear idea of the rights of the soul, and I'll venture next week they'll strike for higher wages. That will be the end of it."

"Will you send the coach-driver to this side of the mills?" asked Kirby, turning to Wolfe.

He spoke kindly: it was his habit to do so. Deborah, seeing the puddler go, crept after him. The three men waited outside. Doctor May walked up and down, chafed. Suddenly he stopped.

"Go back, Mitchell! You say the pocket and the heart of the world speak without meaning to these people. What has its head to say? Taste, culture, refinement? Go!"

Mitchell was leaning against a brick wall. He turned his head indolently, and looked into the mills. There hung about the place a thick, unclean odor. The slightest motion of his hand marked that he perceived it, and his insufferable disgust. That was all. May said nothing, only quickened his angry tramp.

"Besides," added Mitchell, giving a corollary to his answer, "it would be of no use. I am not one of them."

"You do not mean"—said May, facing him.

"Yes, I mean just that. Reform is born of need, not pity. No vital movement of the people's has worked down, for good or evil; fermented, instead, carried up the heaving, cloggy mass. Think back through history, and you will know it. What will this lowest deep— thieves, Magdalens, negroes—do with the light filtered through ponderous Church creeds, Baconian theories, Goethe schemes? Some day, out of their bitter need will be thrown up their own light-bringer,—their Jean Paul, their Cromwell, their Messiah."

"Bah!" was the Doctor's inward criticism. However, in practice, he adopted the theory; for, when, night and morning, afterwards, he prayed that power might be given these degraded souls to rise, he glowed at heart, recognizing an accomplished duty.

Wolfe and the woman had stood in the shadow of the works as the coach drove off. The Doctor had held out his hand in a frank, generous way, telling him to "take care of himself, and to remember it was his right to rise." Mitchell had simply touched his hat, as to an equal, with a quiet look of thorough recognition. Kirby had thrown Deborah some money, which she found, and clutched eagerly enough. They were gone now, all of them. The man sat down on the cinder-road, looking up into the murky sky.

"'T be late, Hugh. Wunnot hur come?"

He shook his head doggedly, and the woman crouched out of his sight against the wall. Do you remember rare moments when a sudden light flashed over yourself, your world, God? when you stood on a mountain-peak, seeing your life as it might have been, as it is? one quick instant, when custom lost its force and every-day usage? when your friend, wife, brother, stood in a new light? your soul was bared, and the grave,—a foretaste of the nakedness of the Judgment-Day? So it came before him, his life, that night. The slow tides of pain he had borne gathered themselves up and surged against his soul. His squalid daily life, the brutal coarseness eating into his brain, as the ashes into his skin: before, these things had been a dull aching into his consciousness; to-night, they were reality. He gripped the filthy red shirt that clung, stiff with soot, about him, and tore it savagely from his arm. The flesh beneath was muddy with grease and ashes,—and the heart beneath that! And the soul? God knows.

Then flashed before his vivid poetic sense the man who had left him,—the pure face, the delicate, sinewy limbs, in harmony with all he knew of beauty or truth. In his cloudy fancy he had pictured a Something like this. He had found it in this Mitchell, even when he idly scoffed at his pain: a Man all-knowing, all-seeing, crowned by Nature, reigning,—the keen glance of his eye falling like a sceptre on other men. And yet his instinct taught him that he too—He! He looked at himself with sudden loathing, sick, wrung his hands with a cry, and then was silent. With all the phantoms of his heated, ignorant fancy, Wolfe had not been vague in his ambitions. They were practical, slowly built up before him out of his knowledge of what he could do. Through years he had day by day made this hope a real thing to himself,—a clear, projected figure of himself, as he might become.

Able to speak, to know what was best, to raise these men and women working at his side up with him: sometimes he forgot this defined hope in the frantic anguish to escape, only to escape,—out of the wet, the pain, the ashes, somewhere, anywhere,—only for one moment of free air on a hill-side, to lie down and let his sick soul throb itself out in the sunshine. But to-night he panted for life. The savage strength of his nature was roused; his cry was fierce to God for justice.

"Look at me!" he said to Deborah, with a low, bitter laugh, striking his puny chest savagely. "What am I worth, Deb? Is it my fault that I am no better? My fault? My fault?"

He stopped, stung with a sudden remorse, seeing her hunchback shape writhing with sobs. For Deborah was crying thankless tears, according to the fashion of women.

"God forgi' me, woman! Things go harder wi' you nor me. It's a worse share."

He got up and helped her to rise; and they went doggedly down the muddy street, side by side.

"It's all wrong," he muttered, slowly,—"all wrong! I dunnot understan'. But it'll end some day."

"Come home, Hugh!" she said, coaxingly; for he had stopped, looking around bewildered.

"Home,—and back to the mill!" He went on saying this over to himself, as if he would mutter down every pain in this dull despair.

She followed him through the fog, her blue lips chattering with cold. They reached the cellar at last. Old Wolfe had been drinking since she went out, and had crept nearer the door. The girl Janey slept heavily in the corner. He went up to her, touching softly the worn white arm with his fingers. Some bitterer thought stung him, as he stood there. He wiped the drops from his forehead, and went into the room beyond, livid, trembling. A hope, trifling, perhaps, but very dear, had died just then out of the poor puddler's life, as he looked at the sleeping, innocent girl,—some plan for the future, in which she had borne a part. He gave it up that moment, then and forever. Only a trifle, perhaps, to us: his face grew a shade paler,—that was all. But, somehow, the man's soul, as God and the angels looked down on it, never was the same afterwards.

Deborah followed him into the inner room. She carried a candle, which she placed on the floor, closing the door after her. She had seen the look on his face, as he turned away: her own grew deadly. Yet, as she came up to him, her eyes glowed. He was seated on an old chest, quiet, holding his face in his hands.

"Hugh!" she said, softly.

He did not speak.

"Hugh, did hur hear what the man said,—him with the clear voice? Did hur hear? Money, money,—that it wud do all?"

He pushed her away,—gently, but he was worn out; her rasping tone fretted him.

"Hugh!"

The candle flared a pale yellow light over the cob-webbed brick walls, and the woman standing there. He looked at her. She was young, in deadly earnest; her faded eyes, and wet, ragged figure caught from their frantic eagerness a power akin to beauty.

"Hugh, it is true! Money ull do it! Oh, Hugh, boy, listen till me! He said it true! It is money!"

"I know. Go back! I do not want you here."

"Hugh, it is t' last time. I'll never worrit hur again."

There were tears in her voice now, but she choked them back:

"Hear till me only to-night! If one of t' witch people wud come, them we heard oft' home, and gif hur all hur wants, what then? Say, Hugh!"

"What do you mean?"

"I mean money."

Her whisper shrilled through his brain.

"If one oft' witch dwarfs wud come from t' lane moors to-night, and gif hur money, to go out,—OUT, I say,—out, lad, where t' sun shines, and t' heath grows, and t' ladies walk in silken gownds, and God stays all t' time,—where t'man lives that talked to us to-night, Hugh knows,—Hugh could walk there like a king!"

He thought the woman mad, tried to check her, but she went on, fierce in her eager haste.

"If *I* were t' witch dwarf, if I had t' money, wud hur thank me? Wud hur take me out o' this place wid hur and Janey? I wud not come into the gran' house hur wud build, to vex hur wid t' hunch,—only at night, when t' shadows were dark, stand far off to see hur."

Mad? Yes! Are many of us mad in this way?

"Poor Deb! poor Deb!" he said, soothingly.

"It is here," she said, suddenly, jerking into his hand a small roll. "I took it! I did it! Me, me!—not hur! I shall be hanged, I shall be burnt in hell, if anybody knows I took it! Out of his pocket, as he leaned against t' bricks. Hur knows?"

She thrust it into his hand, and then, her errand done, began to gather chips together to make a fire, choking down hysteric sobs.

"Has it come to this?"

That was all he said. The Welsh Wolfe blood was honest. The roll was a small green pocket-book containing one or two gold pieces, and a check for an incredible amount, as it seemed to the poor puddler. He laid it down, hiding his face again in his hands.

"Hugh, don't be angry wud me! It's only poor Deb,—hur knows?"

He took the long skinny fingers kindly in his.

"Angry? God help me, no! Let me sleep. I am tired."

He threw himself heavily down on the wooden bench, stunned with pain and weariness. She brought some old rags to cover him.

It was late on Sunday evening before he awoke. I tell God's truth, when I say he had then no thought of keeping this money. Deborah had hid it in his pocket. He found it there. She watched him eagerly, as he took it out.

"I must gif it to him," he said, reading her face.

"Hur knows," she said with a bitter sigh of disappointment. "But it is hur right to keep it."

His right! The word struck him. Doctor May had used the same. He washed himself, and went out to find this man Mitchell. His right! Why did this chance word cling to him so obstinately? Do you hear the fierce devils whisper in his ear, as he went slowly down the darkening street?

The evening came on, slow and calm. He seated himself at the end of an alley leading into one of the larger streets. His brain was clear to-night, keen, intent, mastering. It would not start back, cowardly, from any hellish temptation, but meet it face to face. Therefore the great temptation of his life came to him veiled by no sophistry, but bold, defiant, owning its own vile name, trusting to one bold blow for victory.

He did not deceive himself. Theft! That was it. At first the word sickened him; then he grappled with it. Sitting there on a broken cart-wheel, the fading day, the noisy groups, the church-bells' tolling passed before him like a panorama, while the sharp struggle went on within. This money! He took it out, and looked at it. If he gave it back, what then? He was going to be cool about it.

People going by to church saw only a sickly mill-boy watching them quietly at the alley's mouth. They did not know that he was mad, or they would not have gone by so quietly: mad with hunger; stretching out his hands to the world, that had given so much to them, for leave to live the life God meant him to live. His soul within him was smothering to death; he wanted so much, thought so much, and *knew*—nothing. There was nothing of which he was certain, except the mill and things there. Of God and heaven he had heard so little, that they were to him what fairy-land is to a child: something real, but not here; very far off. His brain, greedy, dwarfed, full of thwarted energy and unused powers, questioned these men and women going by, coldly, bitterly, that night. Was it not his right to live as they,—a pure life, a good, true-hearted life, full of beauty and kind words? He only wanted to know how to use the strength within him. His heart warmed, as he thought of it. He suffered himself to think of it longer. If he took the money?

Then he saw himself as he might be, strong, helpful, kindly. The night crept on, as this one image slowly evolved itself from the crowd of other thoughts and stood triumphant. He looked at it. As he might be! What wonder, if it blinded him to delirium,—the madness that underlies all revolution, all progress, and all fall?

You laugh at the shallow temptation? You see the error underlying its argument so clearly,—that to him a true life was one of full development rather than self-restraint? that he was deaf to the higher tone in a cry of voluntary suffering for truth's sake than in the fullest flow of spontaneous harmony? I do not plead his cause. I only want to show you the mote in my brother's eye: then you can see clearly to take it out.

The money,—there it lay on his knee, a little blotted slip of paper, nothing in itself; used to raise him out of the pit, something straight from God's hand. A thief! Well, what was it to be a thief? He met the question at last, face to face, wiping the clammy drops of sweat from his forehead. God made this money—the fresh air, too—for his children's use. He never made the difference between poor and rich. The Something who looked down on him that moment through the cool gray sky had a kindly face, he knew,—loved his children alike. Oh, he knew that!

There were times when the soft floods of color in the crimson and purple flames, or the clear depth of amber in the water below the bridge, had somehow given him a glimpse of another world than this,—of an infinite depth of beauty and of quiet somewhere,—somewhere, a depth of quiet and rest and love. Looking up now, it became strangely real. The sun had sunk quite below the hills, but his last rays struck upward, touching the zenith. The fog had risen, and the town and river were steeped in its thick, gray damp; but overhead, the sun-touched smoke-clouds opened like a cleft ocean,—shifting, rolling seas of crimson mist, waves of billowy silver veined with blood-scarlet, inner depths unfathomable of glancing light. Wolfe's artist-eye grew drunk with color. The gates of that other world! Fading, flashing before him now! What, in that world of Beauty, Content, and Right, were the petty laws, the mine and thine, of mill-owners and mill-hands?

A consciousness of power stirred within him. He stood up. A man,—he thought, stretching out his hands,—free to work, to live, to love! Free! His right! He folded the scrap of paper in his hand. As his nervous fingers took it in, limp and blotted, so his soul took in the mean temptation, lapped it in fancied rights, in dreams of improved existences, drifting and endless as the cloud-seas of color. Clutching it, as if the tightness of his hold would strengthen his sense of possession, he went aimlessly down the street. It was his watch at the mill. He need not go, need never go again, thank God!—shaking off the thought with unspeakable loathing.

Shall I go over the history of the hours of that

night? how the man wandered from one to another of his old haunts, with a half-consciousness of bidding them farewell,—lanes and alleys and back-yards where the mill-hands lodged,—noting, with a new eagerness, the filth and drunkenness, the pig-pens, the ash-heaps covered with potato-skins, the bloated, pimpled women at the doors, with a new disgust, a new sense of sudden triumph, and, under all, a new, vague dread, unknown before, smothered down, kept under, but still there? It left him but once during the night, when, for the second time in his life, he entered a church. It was a sombre Gothic pile, where the stained light lost itself in far-retreating arches; built to meet the requirements and sympathies of a far other class than Wolfe's. Yet it touched, moved him uncontrollably. The distances, the shadows, the still, marble figures, the mass of silent kneeling worshippers, the mysterious music, thrilled, lifted his soul with a wonderful pain. Wolfe forgot himself, forgot the new life he was going to live, the mean terror gnawing underneath. The voice of the speaker strengthened the charm; it was clear, feeling, full, strong. An old man, who had lived much, suffered much; whose brain was keenly alive, dominant; whose heart was summer-warm with charity. He taught it to-night. He held up Humanity in its grand total; showed the great world-cancer to his people. Who could show it better? He was a Christian reformer; he had studied the age thoroughly; his outlook at man had been free, world-wide, over all time. His faith stood sublime upon the Rock of Ages; his fiery zeal guided vast schemes by which the Gospel was to be preached to all nations. How did he preach it to-night? In burning, light-laden words he painted Jesus, the incarnate Life, Love, the universal Man: words that became reality in the lives of these people,—that lived again in beautiful words and actions, trifling, but heroic. Sin, as he defined it, was a real foe to them; their trials, temptations, were his. His words passed far over the furnace-tender's grasp, toned to suit another class of culture; they sounded in his ears a very pleasant song in an unknown tongue. He meant to cure this world-cancer with a steady eye that had never glared with hunger, and a hand that neither poverty nor strychnine-whiskey had taught to shake. In this morbid, distorted heart of the Welsh puddler he had failed.

Wolfe rose at last, and turned from the church down the street. He looked up; the night had come on foggy, damp; the golden mists had vanished, and the sky lay dull and ash-colored. He wandered again aimlessly down the street, idly wondering what had become of the cloud-sea of crimson and scarlet. The trial-day of this man's life was over, and he had lost the victory. What followed was mere drifting circumstance,—a quicker walking over the path,—that was all. Do you want to hear the end of it? You wish me to make a tragic story out of it? Why, in the police-reports of the morning paper you can find a dozen such tragedies: hints of shipwrecks unlike any that ever befell on the high seas; hints that here a power was lost to heaven,— that there a soul went down where no tide can ebb or flow. Commonplace enough the hints are,—jocose sometimes, done up in rhyme.

Doctor May a month after the night I have told you of, was reading to his wife at breakfast from this fourth column of the morning-paper: an unusual thing,— these police-reports not being, in general, choice reading for ladies; but it was only one item he read.

"Oh, my dear! You remember that man I told you of, that we saw at Kirby's mill?—that was arrested for robbing Mitchell? Here he is; just listen:—'Circuit Court. Judge Day. Hugh Wolfe, operative in Kirby & John's Loudon Mills. Charge, grand larceny. Sentence, nineteen years hard labor in penitentiary. Scoundrel! Serves him right! After all our kindness that night! Picking Mitchell's pocket at the very time!"

His wife said something about the ingratitude of that kind of people, and then they began to talk of something else.

Nineteen years! How easy that was to read! What a simple word for Judge Day to utter! Nineteen years! Half a lifetime!*

Hugh Wolfe sat on the window-ledge of his cell, looking out. His ankles were ironed. Not usual in such cases; but he had made two desperate efforts to escape. "Well," as Haley, the jailer, said, "small blame to him!

---

*Nineteen years was literally half a lifetime. Life expectancy for a male in the 1850s was thirty-seven years. Hugh Wolfe is nineteen years old, for all his "lifetime" in the mills, the "slow heavy years of constant hot work." As was common at the time, he had probably been in the mills since he was nine or ten.

Nineteen years' imprisonment was not a pleasant thing to look forward to." Haley was very good-natured about it, though Wolfe had fought him savagely.

"When he was first caught," the jailer said afterwards, in telling the story, "before the trial, the fellow was cut down at once,—laid there on that pallet like a dead man, with his hands over his eyes. Never saw a man so cut down in my life. Time of the trial, too, came the queerest dodge of any customer I ever had. Would choose no lawyer. Judge gave him one, of course. Gibson it was. He tried to prove the fellow crazy; but it wouldn't go. Thing was plain as daylight: money found on him. 'Twas a hard sentence,—all the law allows; but it was for 'xample's sake. These mill-hands are gettin' onbearable. When the sentence was read, he just looked up, and said the money was his by rights, and that all the world had gone wrong. That night, after the trial, a gentleman came to see him here, name of Mitchell,—him as he stole from. Talked to him for an hour. Thought he came for curiosity, like. After he was gone, thought Wolfe was remarkable quiet, and went into his cell. Found him very low; bed all bloody. Doctor said he had been bleeding at the lungs. He was as weak as a cat; yet if ye'll b'lieve me, he tried to get a-past me and get out. I just carried him like a baby, and threw him on the pallet. Three days after, he tried it again: that time reached the wall. Lord help you! he fought like a tiger,—giv' some terrible blows. Fightin' for life, you see; for he can't live long, shut up in the stone crib down yonder. Got a death-cough now. 'T took two of us to bring him down that day; so I just put the irons on his feet. There he sits, in there. Goin' to-morrow, with a batch more of 'em. That woman, hunchback, tried with him,—you remember?—she's only got three years. 'Complice. But *she's* a woman, you know. He's been quiet ever since I put on irons: giv' up, I suppose. Looks white, sick-lookin'. It acts different on 'em, bein' sentenced. Most of 'em gets reckless, devilish-like. Some prays awful, and sings them vile songs of the mills, all in a breath. That woman, now, she's desper't'. Been beggin' to see Hugh, as she calls him, for three days. I'm a-goin' to let her in. She don't go with him. Here she is in this next cell. I'm a-goin' now to let her in."

He let her in. Wolfe did not see her. She crept into a corner of the cell, and stood watching him. He was scratching the iron bars of the window with a piece of tin which he had picked up, with an idle, uncertain, vacant stare, just as a child or idiot would do.

"Tryin' to get out, old boy?" laughed Haley. "Them irons will need a crow-bar beside your tin, before you can open 'em."

Wolfe laughed, too, in a senseless way.

"I think I'll get out," he said.

"I believe his brain's touched," said Haley, when he came out.

The puddler scraped away with the tin for half an hour. Still Deborah did not speak. At last she ventured nearer, and touched his arm.

"Blood?" she said, looking at some spots on his coat with a shudder.

He looked up at her, "Why, Deb!" he said, smiling,—such a bright, boyish smile, that it went to poor Deborah's heart directly, and she sobbed and cried out loud.

"Oh, Hugh, lad! Hugh! dunnot look at me, when it wur my fault! To think I brought hur to it! And I loved hur so! Oh lad, I dud!"

The confession, even in this wretch, came with the woman's blush through the sharp cry.

He did not seem to hear her,—scraping away diligently at the bars with the bit of tin.

Was he going mad? She peered closely into his face. Something she saw there made her draw suddenly back,—something which Haley had not seen, that lay beneath the pinched, vacant look it had caught since the trial, or the curious gray shadow that rested on it. That gray shadow,—yes, she knew what that meant. She had often seen it creeping over women's faces for months, who died at last of slow hunger or consumption. That meant death, distant, lingering: but this—Whatever it was the woman saw, or thought she saw, used as she was to crime and misery, seemed to make her sick with a new horror. Forgetting her fear of him, she caught his shoulders, and looked keenly, steadily, into his eyes.

"Hugh!" she cried, in a desperate whisper,—"oh, boy, not that! for God's sake, not *that!*"

The vacant laugh went off his face, and he answered her in a muttered word or two that drove her away. Yet the words were kindly enough. Sitting there on his pallet, she cried silently a hopeless sort of tears, but did not speak again. The man looked up furtively at her now and then. Whatever his own trouble was, her distress vexed him with a momentary sting.

It was market-day. The narrow window of the jail looked down directly on the carts and wagons drawn up in a long line, where they had unloaded. He could see, too, and hear distinctly the clink of money as it changed hands, the busy crowd of whites and blacks shoving, pushing one another, and the chaffering and swearing at the stalls. Somehow, the sound, more than anything else had done, wakened him up,—made the whole real to him. He was done with the world and the business of it. He let the tin fall, and looked out, pressing his face close to the rusty bars. How they crowded and pushed! And he,—he should never walk that pavement again! There came Neff Sanders, one of the feeders at the mill, with a basket on his arm. Sure enough, Neff was married the other week. He whistled, hoping he would look up; but he did not. He wondered if Neff remembered he was there,—if any of the boys thought of him up there, and thought that he never was to go down that old cinder-road again. Never again! He had not quite understood it before; but now he did. Not for days or years, but never!—that was it.

How clear the light fell on that stall in front of the market! and how like a picture it was, the dark-green heaps of corn, and the crimson beets, and golden melons! There was another with game: how the light flickered on that pheasant's breast, with the purplish blood dripping over the brown feathers! He could see the red shining of the drops, it was so near. In one minute he could be down there. It was just a step. So easy, as it seemed, so natural to go! Yet it could never be—not in all the thousands of years to come—that he should put his foot on that street again! He thought of himself with a sorrowful pity, as of some one else. There was a dog down in the market, walking after his master with such a stately, grave look!—only a dog, yet he could go backwards and forwards just as he pleased: he had good luck! Why, the very vilest cur, yelping there in the gutter, had not lived his life, had been free to act out whatever thought God had put into his brain; while he—No, he would not think of that! He tried to put the thought away, and to listen to a dispute between a countryman and a woman about some meat; but it would come back. He, what had he done to bear this?

Then came the sudden picture of what might have been, and now. He knew what it was to be in the penitentiary, how it went with men there. He knew how in these long years he should slowly die, but not until soul and body had become corrupt and rotten,—how, when he came out, if he lived to come, even the lowest of the mill-hands would jeer him,—how his hands would be weak, and his brain senseless and stupid. He believed he was almost that now. He put his hand to his head, with a puzzled, weary look. It ached, his head, with thinking. He tried to quiet himself. It was only right, perhaps; he had done wrong. But was there right or wrong for such as he? What was right? And who had ever taught him? He thrust the whole matter away.

A dark, cold quiet crept through his brain. It was all wrong; but let it be! It was nothing to him more than the others. Let it be!

The door grated, as Haley opened it.

"Come, my woman! Must lock up for t' night. Come, stir yerself!"

She went up and took Hugh's hand.

"Good-night, Deb," he said, carelessly.

She had not hoped he would say more; but the tired pain on her mouth just then was bitterer than death. She took his passive hand and kissed it.

"Hur'll never see Deb again!" she ventured, her lips growing colder and more bloodless.

What did she say that for? Did he not know it? Yet he would not be impatient with poor old Deb. She had trouble of her own, as well as he.

"No, never again," he said, trying to be cheerful.

She stood just a moment, looking at him. Do you laugh at her, standing there, with her hunchback, her rags, her bleared, withered face, and the great despised love tugging at her heart?

"Come, you!" called Haley, impatiently.

She did not move.

"Hugh!" she whispered.

It was to be her last word. What was it?

"Hugh, boy, not *THAT*!"

He did not answer. She wrung her hands, trying to be silent, looking in his face in an agony of entreaty. He smiled again, kindly.

"It is best, Deb. I cannot bear to be hurted any more."

"Hur knows," she said, humbly.

"Tell my father good-bye; and—and kiss little Janey."

She nodded, saying nothing, looked in his face again, and went out of the door. As she went, she staggered.

"Drinkin' to-day?" broke out Haley, pushing her before him. "Where the Devil did you get it? Here, in with ye!" and he shoved her into her cell, next to Wolfe's, and shut the door.

Along the wall of her cell there was a crack low down by the floor, through which she could see the light from Wolfe's. She had discovered it days before. She hurried in now, and, kneeling down by it, listened, hoping to hear some sound. Nothing but the rasping of the tin on the bars. He was at his old amusement again. Something in the noise jarred on her ear, for she shivered as she heard it. Hugh rasped away at the bars. A dull old bit of tin, not fit to cut korl with.

He looked out of the window again. People were leaving the market now. A tall mulatto girl, following her mistress, her basket on her head, crossed the street just below, and looked up. She was laughing; but, when she caught sight of the haggard face peering out through the bars, suddenly grew grave, and hurried by. A free, firm step, a clear-cut olive face, with a scarlet turban tied on one side, dark, shining eyes, and on the head the basket poised, filled with fruit and flowers, under which the scarlet turban and bright eyes looked out half-shadowed. The picture caught his eye. It was good to see a face like that. He would try to-morrow, and cut one like it. *To-morrow!* He threw down the tin, trembling, and covered his face with his hands. When he looked up again, the daylight was gone.

Deborah, crouching near by on the other side of the wall, heard no noise. He sat on the side of the low pallet, thinking. Whatever was the mystery which the woman had seen on his face, it came out now slowly, in the dark there, and became fixed,—a something never seen on his face before. The evening was darkening fast. The market had been over for an hour; the rumbling of the carts over the pavement grew more infrequent: he listened to each, as it passed, because he thought it was to be for the last time. For the same reason, it was, I suppose, that he strained his eyes to catch a glimpse of each passer-by, wondering who they were, what kind of homes they were going to, if they had children,—listening eagerly to every chance word in the street, as if— (God be merciful to the man! what strange fancy was this?)—as if he never should hear human voices again.

It was quite dark at last. The street was a lonely one. The last passenger, he thought, was gone. No,—there was a quick step: Joe Hill, lighting the lamps. Joe was a good old chap; never passed a fellow without some joke or other. He remembered once seeing the place where he lived with his wife. "Granny Hill" the boys called her. Bedridden she was; but so kind as Joe was to her! kept the room so clean!—and the old woman, when he was there, was laughing at some of "t' lad's foolishness." The step was far down the street; but he could see him place the ladder, run up, and light the gas. A longing seized him to be spoken to once more.

"Joe!" he called, out of the grating. "Good-bye, Joe!"

The old man stopped a moment, listening uncertainly; then hurried on. The prisoner thrust his hand out of the window, and called again, louder; but Joe was too far down the street. It was a little thing; but it hurt him,—this disappointment.

"Good-bye, Joe!" he called, sorrowfully enough.

"Be quiet!" said one of the jailers, passing the door, striking on it with his club.

Oh, that was the last, was it?

There was an inexpressible bitterness on his face, as he lay down on the bed, taking the bit of tin, which he had rasped to a tolerable degree of sharpness, in his hand,—to play with, it may be. He bared his arms, looking intently at their corded veins and sinews. Deborah, listening in the next cell, heard a slight clicking sound, often repeated. She shut her lips tightly, that she might not scream; the cold drops of sweat broke over her, in her dumb agony.

"Hur knows best," she muttered at last, fiercely clutching the boards where she lay.

If she could have seen Wolfe, there was nothing about him to frighten her. He lay quite still, his arms outstretched, looking at the pearly stream of moonlight coming into the window. I think in that one hour that came then he lived back over all the years that had gone before. I think that all the low, vile life, all his wrongs, all his starved hopes, came then, and stung him with a farewell poison that made him sick unto death. He made neither moan nor cry, only turned his worn face now and then to the pure light, that seemed so far off, as one that said, "How long, O Lord? how long?"

The hour was over at last. The moon, passing over her nightly path, slowly came nearer, and threw the light across his bed on his feet. He watched it steadily, as it crept up, inch by inch, slowly. It seemed to him to carry with it a great silence. He had been so hot and tired there always in the mills! The years had been so fierce and cruel! There was coming now quiet and coolness and sleep. His tense limbs relaxed, and settled in a calm languor. The blood ran fainter and slow from his heart. He did not think now with a savage anger of what might be and was not; he was conscious only of deep stillness creeping over him. At first he saw a sea of faces: the mill-men,—women he had known, drunken and bloated,—Janeys timid and pitiful,—poor old Debs: then they floated together like a mist, and faded away, leaving only the clear, pearly moonlight.

Whether, as the pure light crept up the stretched-out figure, it brought with it calm and peace, who shall say? His dumb soul was alone with God in judgment. A Voice may have spoken for it from far-off Calvary, "Father, forgive them, for they know not what they do!" Who dare say? Fainter and fainter the heart rose and fell, slower and slower the moon floated from behind a cloud, until, when at last its full tide of white splendor swept over the cell, it seemed to wrap and fold into a deeper stillness the dead figure that never should move again. Silence deeper than the Night! Nothing that moved, save the black, nauseous stream of blood dripping slowly from the pallet to the floor!

There was outcry and crowd enough in the cell the next day. The coroner and his jury, the local editors, Kirby himself, and boys with their hands thrust knowingly into their pockets and heads on one side, jammed into the corners. Coming and going all day. Only one woman. She came late, and outstayed them all. A Quaker, or Friend, as they call themselves. I think this woman was known by that name in heaven. A homely body, coarsely dressed in gray and white. Deborah (for Haley had let her in) took notice of her. She watched them all—sitting on the end of the pallet, holding his head in her arms with the ferocity of a watch-dog, if any of them touched the body. There was no meekness, no sorrow, in her face; the stuff out of which murderers are made, instead. All the time Haley and the woman were laying straight the limbs and cleaning the cell, Deborah sat still, keenly watching the Quaker's face. Of all the crowd there that day, this woman alone had not spoken to her,—only once or twice had put some cordial to her lips. After they all were gone, the woman, in the same still, gentle way, brought a vase of wood-leaves and berries, and placed it by the pallet, then opened the narrow window. The fresh air blew in, and swept the woody fragrance over the dead face. Deborah looked up with a quick wonder.

"Did hur know my boy wud like it? Did hur know Hugh?"

"I know Hugh now."

The white fingers passed in a slow, pitiful way over the dead, worn face. There was a heavy shadow in the quiet eyes.

"Did hur know where they'll bury Hugh?" said Deborah in a shrill tone, catching her arm.

This had been the question hanging on her lips all day.

"In t' town-yard? Under t' mud and ash? T' lad'll smother, woman! He wur born in t' lane moor, where t' air is frick and strong. Take hur out, for God's sake, take hur out where t' air blows!"

The Quaker hesitated, but only for a moment. She put her strong arm around Deborah and led her to the window.

"Thee sees the hills, friend, over the river? Thee sees how the light lies warm there, and the winds of God blow all the day? I live there,—where the blue smoke is, by the trees. Look at me." She turned Deborah's face to her own, clear and earnest. "Thee will believe me? I will take Hugh and bury him there to-morrow."

Deborah did not doubt her. As the evening wore on, she leaned against the iron bars, looking at the hills that rose far off, through the thick sodden clouds, like a bright, unattainable calm. As she looked, a shadow of their solemn repose fell on her face; its fierce discontent faded into a pitiful, humble quiet. Slow, solemn tears gathered in her eyes: the poor weak eyes turned so hopelessly to the place where Hugh was to rest, the grave heights looking higher and brighter and more solemn than ever before. The Quaker watched her keenly. She came to her at last, and touched her arm.

"When thee comes back," she said, in a low, sorrowful tone, like one who speaks from a strong heart deeply moved with remorse or pity, "thee shall begin thy life again,—there on the hills. I came too late; but not for thee,—by God's help, it may be."

Not too late. Three years after, the Quaker began her work. I end my story here. At evening-time it was light. There is no need to tire you with the long years of sunshine, and fresh air, and slow, patient Christ-love, needed to make healthy and hopeful this impure body and soul. There is a homely pine house, on one of these hills, whose windows overlook broad, wooded slopes and clover-crimsoned meadows,—niched into the very place where the light is warmest, the air freest. It is the Friends' meeting-house. Once a week they sit there, in their grave, earnest way, waiting for the Spirit of Love to speak, opening their simple hearts to receive His words. There is a woman, old, deformed, who takes a humble place among them: waiting like them: in her gray dress, her worn face, pure and meek, turned now and then to the sky. A woman much loved by these silent, restful people; more silent than they, more humble, more loving. Waiting: with her eyes turned to hills higher and purer than these on which she lives, dim and far off now, but to be reached some day. There may be in her heart some latent hope to meet there the love denied her here,—that she shall find him whom she lost, and that then she will not be all-unworthy. Who blames her? Something is lost in the passage of every soul from one eternity to the other,—something pure and beautiful, which might have been and was not: a hope, a talent, a love, over which the soul mourns, like

Esau deprived of his birthright. What blame to the meek Quaker, if she took her lost hope to make the hills of heaven more fair?

Nothing remains to tell that the poor Welsh puddler once lived, but this figure of the mill-woman cut in korl. I have it here in a corner of my library. I keep it hid behind a curtain,—it is such a rough, ungainly thing. Yet there are about it touches, grand sweeps of outline, that show a master's hand. Sometimes,—to-night, for instance,—the curtain is accidentally drawn back, and I see a bare arm stretched out imploringly in the darkness, and an eager, wolfish face watching mine: a wan, woful face, through which the spirit of the dead korl-cutter looks out, with its thwarted life, its mighty hunger, its unfinished work. Its pale, vague lips seem to tremble with a terrible question. "Is this the End?" they say,—"nothing beyond? no more?" Why, you tell me you have seen that look in the eyes of dumb brutes,—horses dying under the lash. I know.

The deep of the night is passing while I write. The gas-light wakens from the shadows here and there the objects which lie scattered through the room: only faintly, though; for they belong to the open sunlight. As I glance at them, they each recall some task or pleasure of the coming day. A half-moulded child's head; Aphrodite; a bough of forest-leaves; music; work; homely fragments, in which lie the secrets of all eternal truth and beauty. Prophetic all! Only this dumb, woful face seems to belong to and end with the night. I turn to look at it. Has the power of its desperate need commanded the darkness away? While the room is yet steeped in heavy shadow, a cool, gray light suddenly touches its head like a blessing hand, and its groping arm points through the broken cloud to the far East, where, in the flickering, nebulous crimson, God has set the promise of the Dawn.

# A BIOGRAPHICAL INTERPRETATION

*Life in the Iron Mills* was not written out of compassion or condescending pity. The thirty-year-old Rebecca Harding who wrote it, wrote in absolute identification with "thwarted, wasted lives . . . mighty hungers . . . unawakened power"; despised love; circumstances that denied use of capacities; imperfect, self-tutored art that could have only odd moments for its doing—as if these were her own. And they were, however differently embodied in the life of a daughter of the privileged class.

It was in front of the Harding house that the long trains of mules dragged their masses of pig iron and the slow stream of human life crept past, night and morning, year after year, to work their fourteen-hour days six days a week. The little girl who observed it grew into womanhood, into spinsterhood, still at the window in that house, and the black industrial smoke was her daily breath.

The town was Wheeling, on the Ohio, in the border slave state of what was then Virginia. When the Harding family moved there in 1836 (Rebecca was five), it was one of only a handful of steel towns in the nation. All her growing years, the slave South, the free North; the industrial future, the agrarian present, the wilderness that was once all the past—were uniquely commingled here. In the streets, farmers were as familiar a sight as Irish and Cornish steelworkers, slaves, free blacks, commercial travelers, bargemen, draymen, Indians, and rawboned mountain people in to work at the mills. Over the country's single north-south National Road, snaking mostly through wilderness to this halting point, came huge vans with cotton bales for Northern mills, manufactures for the South; stagecoaches carrying passengers to and from the river boats that connected St. Louis and New Orleans with the East; and Conestoga wagons with emigrants or immigrants still in European dress, heading west. And over all, through the night and morning river mists, the constant changes of light, was a sense of vast unpeopled distance from the hills that curved fold on fold far as eye could see.

"These sights and sounds did not come common to her." The slow-moving thoughtful Rebecca absorbed them into herself with the quiet intensity that marked all her confrontation with life, and with an unshared sense of wonder, of mystery.

She was the eldest of five children. Her father, a successful businessman, later City Treasurer, professedly hated "vulgar American life" and its world of business, secluding himself evenings for what he did love: reading Elizabethan literature, mostly Shakespeare.

"He was English and homesick," Rebecca wrote of him years later. "We were not intimate with him as with our mother."[1] The household revolved around him. Her mother ("the most accurate historian I ever knew, with enough knowledge to outfit a dozen modern college-educated women") was kept busy with an ever increasing family and running the large household noiselessly.

It was a house that had servants, perhaps slaves, for necessary tasks. Public schools did not yet exist. Rebecca's mother did the early teaching, and later there were occasional tutors, usually brought in for her brothers. Rebecca rambled; she read. The books (Maria Edgeworth, Bunyan, Scott) were of a remote world of pilgrims, knights and ladies, magic, crusaders. But once, in her soot-specked cherry tree hideout, in a new collection of *Moral Tales* (it was years before she discovered the anonymous author was Hawthorne), she found three unsigned stories about an ordinary American town, everyday sights and sounds, the rambles of a little girl like herself. She read and re-read them so often that "I know almost every line of them by heart, even now." In them her own secret feelings, so opposite to those of her complex, austere father, were verified: that "the commonplace folk and things which I saw every day had mystery and charm . . . belonged to the magic world [of books] as much as knights and pilgrims."

When she was fourteen (an age when most Wheeling girls had already been working in the mills or as domestic slaveys for years), Rebecca was sent—not too far away—to live with her mother's sister in Washington, Pennsylvania, to attend the three-year Female Seminary there and be "finished."

"Of all cursed places under the sun, where the hungriest soul can hardly pick up a few grains of knowledge," Olive Schreiner writes of that century, "a girls' boarding-school is the worst. . . . They finish everything but imbecility and weakness, and that they cultivate. They are nicely adapted machines for experimenting on the question, 'Into how little space a human soul can be crushed?'"[2]

Probably the indictment is too severe in this instance, but certainly it was not an atmosphere conducive to learning, development, attainment. The ardent "hunger to know" (later ascribed to Hugh Wolfe and other of her fictional people) was already deep in Rebecca. She was eager for companions, for stimulus, exploration, range, substance.

Little of substance beyond religion and "soft attractive graces" was offered the young ladies. "Enough math to do accounts, enough astronomy to point out constellations, a little music and drawing, and French, history, literature at discretion" is how Rebecca describes it.

Nor did she find satisfactory companionship. For all her classmates' shocked delight at her irreverent wit, Rebecca's very seriousness of purpose and "hunger to know" set her apart.

Still it was a larger world than home. It was a college town, site of the (all male, of course) Washington College. There were more books, more current literature available. Speakers came through regularly on the college circuit, and sometimes Seminary girls were permitted to attend. There was a bracing sense of currents and concerns of the time, and the stimulation of hearing famous figures, such as Horace Greeley.

And there was Francis LeMoyne, the town physician, radical reformer, abolitionist (their national vice-presidential candidate in 1840), agnostic. "He should have lived in a . . . great arena. . . . He had the power for any work."[3] Unquestionably, the most challenging experience of those years was her acquaintance with him.

This "uncouth mass of flesh," "mad against Destiny, . . . [stumbling] blindly against unconquerable ills," "smothered rights and triumphant wrongs," "inflamed with the needs and sufferings of . . . countless lives" brought to Rebecca a troubling sense of "a gulf of pain and wrong . . . the under-life of America," and deepened her childhood feeling of something of great mystery and portent in this "vulgar" everyday American life.

Fourteen years later, in her first novel, *Margret Howth*, she was still trying to come to terms with the meaning of LeMoyne's radical life and beliefs, so diametrically opposed to the precepts and assumptions of her own upbringing.

She graduated as valedictorian, still hungry to know. The "larger life" away from home was over. It was 1848. She was seventeen. Even had she wanted to go on with education, there was but one college in the entire country that would admit a female, the scandalous, unthinkable (abolitionist) Oberlin. The massed social structure prescribed one sphere, one vocation for a woman of her class: domestic—marriage, or serving as daughter, sister, aunt where needed. Only in case of extreme economic necessity did a girl or woman of her circle live away from home, with but one "respectable" occupation open to her—teaching (at a third of a man's pay).

That summer, a few hundred miles north at Seneca Falls, the first women's rights convention in the world was being held. Their Declaration spoke of the situation of women as:

> a history of repeated injuries and usurpations of the part of man toward woman. . . . He has monopolized nearly all profitable employments, and from those she is permitted to follow, she receives but a scanty remuneration. He closes against her all avenues to wealth and distinction which he considers most honorable to himself. . . . He has denied her the facilities for obtaining a thorough education, all colleges being closed against her. . . . He has endeavored, in every way that he could, to destroy her confidence in her own powers, to lessen her self-respect, and make her willing to lead a dependent and abject life.

It is doubtful that Rebecca read the Declaration. Even if she had, it is doubtful that the seventeen-year-old girl would have accepted it as a description of her circumstance. To her, it was personal, singular; something awry, unnatural *in her* to harbor needs, interests, longings for which there seemed no place or way or precedent.

She was a dark, vigorous, sturdily built girl, with a full, handsome, strong-jawed face that decades later was to become the most admired, sketched, photographed face of its generation in the person of her famous son Richard.[4] In her own time, when what was prized in female features was delicacy, her appearance was probably considered unfortunate—for a girl. Her manner was direct, "unvarnished," quiet.

The Wheeling to which she returned, and in which she was to be immured for the next thirteen years, was not Boston, nor Amherst, nor Concord—nor even Washington, Pennsylvania, with college circuit lectures, traveling theater, a Francis LeMoyne. It was a yeasty, booming industrial town of nearly 13,000 people, but with no intellectual or literary circles of any kind. The fever for gold, just beginning in California, had long dominated here; the heavy industrial smoke, manifesting its own kind of gold dust, pervaded more than the atmosphere.

The social life open to Rebecca in her own class was with young men intent on making the most of the possibilities for "getting on," and with young women whose concern—natural under the circumstances of but one sanctioned vocation—was with getting asked into the most advantageous possible marriage. All social activities were calculated toward these ends. Rebecca did not involve herself in the expected social round.

Whatever the reasons were—subtle family ones,[5] the lonely pull of obviously unshared interests—among them must have been Rebecca's refusal to remain in situations of emptiness, of falsity, of injuries to her sense of selfhood—where there was choice. She stayed almost exclusively within the family circle.

As the eldest daughter in a large household, even one with servants, there was much help to be given her mother in the commonplace, necessary tasks of caring for family needs, younger children; keeping the atmosphere pleasant, especially for her father. The bonds of love were strong—she writes of "the protection and peace of home"—but they were not bonds of mutuality. She had to keep her longings, questionings, insurrections, secret.

She could not even freely discuss literature. She had come home excited over living native writers. "We were in the first flush of our triumph in the beginnings of a national literature. . . . these new men—Holmes and Lowell and Hawthorne—were our own, the indigenous growth of the soil." To her father, all literature had ended with Shakespeare; the United States was incapable of culture. No other viewpoint was expressible.

Nor was there any of LeMoyne's concern with "the unhelped pain of life." All through the fifties—that earthquake decade of anti-slavery, bleeding Kansas, women's rights, the fugitive slave law, Dred Scott, John Brown, the struggle for a ten-hour workday—her family and its circle stayed removed, indifferent, when not hostile. Except through reading, Rebecca was shut in their narrowness. She tells of one family, "radicals, believers in divorce and women's rights, refusing to eat sugar or use cotton, visited once by John Brown," who (naturally) were "social outcasts." Rebecca did not question the taboo.

Thirteen years are to go by before the seventeen-year-old girl-valedictorian emerges as the thirty-year-old author of *Life in the Iron Mills*. Shrouded years. The outward, known facts are so few, it is to the writings one must turn to piece together what some of those thirteen years must have been.

In Rebecca's first published fiction, there is a gallery of girls before marriage, devoted to their families, especially their usually difficult fathers. They are "hungry to make some use of themselves, . . . undergoing fierce struggles to tame and bind to some unfitting work, the power within."[6] They responsibly carry out household tasks "though heart and brain need more than this." Unlike those dear to them, they are "hurt" by

> the filth, injustice, bafflings in the world. . . . she [Dode] never glossed them over as "necessity," or shirked them as we do: she cried hot, weak tears, for instance, over the wrongs of the slaves about her, her old father's ignorance, her own cramped life. . . . these passion-fits were the only events of her life.

Throughout her work, there is another recurrent figure: proud, vulnerable young women, subjected to indignities and rejection because their appearance and being do not fit the prevailing standards of female beauty or behavior. Young men say to them patronizingly: "You are built for use, but not for show." They are made to feel shame for their energy and strength, which "they cannot remember to dissemble into fragility that appeals." They are penalized because they cannot "blush and flutter and plume themselves when a man comes near." They are "freaks" for their "rare sincerity" or "seriousness."

If they attract, they at the same time repel:

> He took her short, thick hand in his delicate fingers, but dropped it again quickly. The fiery spirit in his veins rose to meet the heat in hers . . . but he really could not bear to see a young girl with a paw shaped like a man's.

When they love, it is in an agony of intensity—love most often unspoken, or despised; or if mutual, having to be denied.

There are older women, realizing that theirs is to be the social obloquy of the unchosen, the unmarried, "loathing themselves as one whom God had thought unworthy of every women's right—to love and be loved, . . . their strength drying up within them, jeered at, utterly alone." "We laugh at their trial," Rebecca goes on to say. "I think the quick fagots at the stake were fitter subjects for laughter." Like the younger women, they school themselves to maintain dignity, integrity; they armor, imprison themselves in "the great power of reticence."

There is nothing sexless about them. They suffer physically as well as socially. Their "hopeless thirst is freshly bitter." Margret Howth "kindles at the look or touch" of the man she unrequitedly loves "as if her veins were filled with subtle flame."

With Rebecca's younger women, they comprise the most openly physical women in the fiction of the time. Here is a bride-to-be, dressing up as the month of June, "the moist warm month," for a costume party:

> Some tranced summer's day might have drowsed down into such a human form . . . on the thick grass-crusted meadows. There was the full contour of the limbs hid under warm green folds, the white flesh that glowed when you touched it as if some smothered heat lay beneath, the snaring eyes, the sleeping face, the amber hair uncoiled in a languid quiet, while yellow jasmines deepened its hue into molten sunshine, and a great tiger-lily laid its sultry head on her breast.

And always there is the vein of "unused powers, thwarted energies, starved hopes"; the hunger for a life more abundant than in women's sanctioned sphere—in the full human context of Hugh Wolfe's definition: "A true life is one of full development of faculties."

Clues? Autobiography? Of a sort. There is enough correspondence to outward fact, and what was not experienced directly went deep enough to be carefully and caringly recorded.

But of what is most singular in those thirteen years—the development of that girl in her cramped life, fiercely struggling to tame and bind to some unfitting work the power within; of what made it a cramped life; of how she faced down the harm and maimings of her personal situation, the self-scorn, the thwartings, and—fitted in between tasks and family needs, in secret and in isolation, without literary friendship and its encouragement—developed an ear, a discipline, made of herself a writer, *against the prevalent, found her own subject*—of this there is scarcely a word.

The "hunger to know" and for "summat to make her live" must have gone on, unsatisfied. Like Emily Dickinson, in withdrawing from the social round she created some measure of time for herself beyond the inescapable family pulls and responsibilities; and she was of those rare fortunate who had "a room of one's own." When her brother Wilson went to Washington College—where, unlike the Female Seminary, the courses had to have substance and range—she set herself to studying the books and subjects she had not had, giving herself his lessons. Then that too was over. She writes somewhere of "the curse of an education one cannot use."

She continued to read avidly. But books, for all their companionship, could only have intensified the sense of constriction, of waste, of the unattainable. Like the young Harriet Beecher at the same age, "thought, intense emotional thought, became a disease."[7]

Almost the first sentence in *Life in the Iron Mills* is: "I open the window, and looking out . . ." She must have opened her window and looked out at the life beyond her a great deal in those years. Year after year, she saw changes: the factories and mills spreading over more and more of the landscape, thieving the farms; the coming of the first railroad, the Baltimore & Ohio; coal mine smoke beginning to stain the once pure mists over the Appalachians; the Ohio River darkening with wastes; the throngs and traffic in the streets, thickening; and always, night and morning, the workers on their way to or from the mills.

And she walked. Not the carefree rambles of childhood, for she was encumbered now by the steel-ribbed corsets and dragging skirts of her sex and class,[8] the restrictions as to where she might go and how she must behave. She walked in stupor, in vacancy, in self-scorn; walking off a "passion-fit" or seeking release from the walls of family; in joy of motion, the one active exercise of a lady's body permissible, or "in an ecstasy of awareness . . . in the peopled maze of the streets." Walking was her travel, her adventure, her transaction with the world—living substance for her idling intellect and imagination. It is significant that much of *Life in the Iron Mills* and *Margret Howth* takes place during walks.

At some point she began secretly, seriously, to write. Whatever the roots, all might have fallen away into silence as with nearly all women before her, but the times were nurturing. Writing was being demonstrated as the one profession it was possible to carry on within the sphere, the one male domain in which there was beginning to be undeniable, even conspicuous, success by women. The upswelling women's rights movement had created an atmosphere, a challenge, an interest.

Eighteen hundred and fifty, the year Rebecca was nineteen, began the decade called by literary historians "the feminine fifties."[9] Two years before, *Jane Eyre* had appeared, with its unprecedented heroine who was *plain* and earned her own living and was rebelliously conscious of unused powers, restrictions because of her sex. Harriet Beecher Stowe's *Uncle Tom's Cabin*, which reached and affected more readers the world over than any work of fiction before (or since), came out in 1852. Grace Greenwood and Fanny Fern (Sara Willis Parton), joined later by the devastating Gail Hamilton, were earning splendid and well-publicized incomes with their writing. Parton's *Ruth Hall* (1855) stunned readers, including an admiring Hawthorne, with its account of the struggles of a woman genius against poverty and prejudice. For the first time, year after year, there were successful novels by women. Contrary to received opinion, in its first high tide this feminine writing was predominantly serious—about some-thing—not romantic fluff or sentimental slush.

The ardor, "the fierce thirst for beauty, to know it, to create it, to be something other than [she] was," turned in this direction. At first, Rebecca says, she "rashly" tried her hand at "idylls delicately tinted . . . heroines in white dresses that never need washing . . . deep-dyed villains, full-blooded saints . . . dark conspiracies, women rare and radiant in Italian bowers." "I never was there," she says. "I am willing to do my best, but I live in the commonplace."

She *chose* to live in the commonplace, this common-place that was nowhere in books. Her changing changing Wheeling, the huge mills, the new men of power, owners, managers, whom she observed obliquely in her father's house; the despised, ignored life she saw from her windows, mingled among in the streets; "filth, injustice, bafflings," "vulgar American life"; all those years of seeming vacancy and waste, they had drawn her more and more with LeMoyne's sense of great portent, great meaning, hid within them.

Now in this dazzling possibility of expression, use, she came to this as subject. Without realizing it, she had the advantage of the writer's deepest questions: what is happening here, what does this mean? Of the "massed, vile, slimy lives" she asked, "Is that all of their lives? nothing beneath? all?"

But this "commonplace" was outside the permitted sphere. She was house-bound, class-bound, sex-bound; there was no way of natural, direct (participatory) access to the worlds of work and power for her.

It is almost impossible for us at a later, freer time, to conceive the difficulties of accumulating the dense accretion of significant details out of which *Life in the Iron Mills* springs so terribly to life (details that could come no more out of books than does Wolfe, or for that matter, Clarke, Kirby, May, Mitchell).

Perhaps only once was Rebecca able to take Deborah's night walk to the "city of fires"; she would not have been permitted to go unescorted, or to linger, or to initiate or participate too actively in any conversation. In homes such as the Hardings', labor relations, politics, gritty subjects, were not discussed around the ladies socially. How did she come then by the observation, the knowledge, of the incomparable rainy night mill scene with its seizing descriptions and its unequaled encompassing of various class attitudes? How, too, did she come to know the fetid kennel-like room where the Wolfes lived, with its slimy moss-covered earth floor; and the dress, the differing talk and *beings* of its potato eaters?

She must have had to use "trespass vision," eavesdrop, ponder everything, dwell within it with all the resources of intellect and imagination; literally make of herself (in Henry James' famous phrase) "one on whom nothing is lost." Each walk, each encounter, had to be freighted with significance, each opportunity for knowing seized. More, with demeaning, painful, excited strategem, she must have had to *create* opportunities for knowledge; and for a knowing relationship with those outside the bounds of her class.

And in the process, the noting of reality was transformed into comprehension, Vision.

In *Margret Howth*, she writes of Lo (Lois), a black peddlar girl, crippled in a cotton mill accident:

> . . . this creature, that Nature had thrown impatiently aside as a failure, so marred, imperfect . . . came strangely near to her [Margret], claimed recognition by some subtile instinct . . . some strange sympathy drew her to this poor wretch, dwarfed, alone in the world,—some tie of equality.

*Some tie of equality*, of kinship. The subtle recognition that these were not of a lower order, but human beings like herself, capable of—with the right to— denied circumstances for full development. As Hugh saw himself, she saw them. *As they might be.*

Her father had maintained that tragedy could have

only to do with the noble, the high born. But she recognized that this misuse of human beings by industry was tragedy, "terrible tragedy, a reality of soul (and body) starvation, of living death." And "in its very extremity, the most solemn prophecy which the world had known of the Hope to come." *As they might be.*

"I want to make it a real thing for you. . . . You, busy in making straight paths for your feet on the hills."

It may have taken her years to embody her vision. "Hewing and hacking," like Hugh, "working at one figure for months and, when it was finished, breaking it to pieces in a fit of disappointment." Writing, discarding, trying again. Often the effort and the transport must have seemed a kind of insanity, a vain delusion. There was nothing or no one outside herself to verify or justify it. Only the Vision, and the need to make it a real thing.

When at last it was done, she did not know what to call it: a story? a parable? an article? It was not like any of these. Furthermore, the only magazine she could think of that might possibly publish something so different was also the most unlikely: *The Atlantic Monthly*, the most prestigious, influential magazine of the day.[10] Revered by readers and writers alike, the great of the time, Emerson, Thoreau, Lowell, Stowe, Holmes, Whittier, appeared regularly in it. But it also published odd things, new things; had indicated it would welcome material dealing with "real life"; and had shown friendliness to women—rights and writers. Rebecca sent the piece there.

A letter came back in January 1861. She carried it around "half a day without opening it, being so sure it would be a refusal." Instead it was a laudatory acceptance, signed for the editorial board by the publisher himself, James T. Fields. Fifty dollars—a huge sum then—was enclosed in payment, the first paid earnings of all her thirty years.

They had but a single suggestion for change: the name of the "story" was not "taking" enough. In that case, Rebecca wrote back, the *article* could be called "The Korl Woman" or "Beyond"; but she still preferred "Life in the Iron Mills." And that her name not be revealed as author. No hint of the tumult of joy she must have felt at their acceptance, the sense of vindication of years of solitary effort. The great power of reticence managed two sentences: "Your letter is kind, and gave me much pleasure," and "I thank you for your encouragement."

They wrote back, again lauding the story. They wanted more work; they wanted exclusive rights to everything she wrote; they offered $100 at once toward anything she might write in the future.

"I see that the novelty of the scene of the story has made you overestimate me; another most probably would disappoint you." As for the advance, no. "If I were writing with a hundred dollar bill before me, the article would be broad and deep just $100 and no more—dollarish all over."

She did not say that in a fever of work, wrought up by the confirming recognition and by the possibility of further publication, she was writing (or perhaps had gone back to writing) something else—a longer, more ambitious piece that would give her greater scope. Hugh Wolfe's cry (her cry), "Wrong, it's all wrong," was again to be authenticated; the portent and vision of *Life in the Iron Mills* made more manifest; the tie of equality made flesh and blood. There was still the troubling, radical figure of Francis LeMoyne, who thirteen years ago had given her her first awareness of the gulf of pain and wrong outside herself, who had insisted that work for change was the only worthy way to live. The dialogues between LeMoyne and her father had gone on in her head all these years; she would translate them into fiction. And there were the "new men" of power to be more fully delineated; and love, female sacrifice, the embittering scorn and unknowingness of society toward women not yet married, all to be written.

The three-hundred-page novel, *A Story of Today* (afterward called *Margret Howth*), was near completion when *Life in the Iron Mills* appeared.

To the readers of that April 1861 *Atlantic*, *Life in the Iron Mills* came as absolute News, with the shock of unprepared-for revelation.

In the consciousness of literary America, there had been no dark satanic mills;[11] outside of slavery, no myriads of human beings whose lives were "terrible tragedy . . . a reality of soul starvation, of living death." When industry was considered at all, it was as an invasion of pastoral harmony, a threat of materialism to the *spirit*. If working people existed—and nowhere were they material for serious attention, let alone central subject[12]—they were "clean-haired Yankee mill girls," "mind[s] among the spindles," or Whitman's

workwomen and workmen of these States having your own divine and strong life . . .[13]

"Life lies about us dumb," Emerson had written. "How few materials are yet used by our arts. The mass of creatures and of qualities are still hid and expectant." This reality, hitherto "dumb . . . secret in the nightmare fog," verified him beyond expectation with its crowding of implications, troublings, its new themes and types, images, sounds, smells, dictions.

It was an instant sensation; it was recognized as a literary landmark. A wide and distinguished audience, shaken by its power and original vision, spoke of it as a work of genius.

Far off in her native Wheeling, little of this acclaim reached Rebecca. Forwarded letters began to arrive, but her first real indication of the impact her work was having came with a note from Hawthorne, Hawthorne himself, the author of those three anonymous tales she had memorized as a child. He was in Washington, would be going on to Harpers Ferry, and might he come on from there to meet her?

"Well, I suppose Esther felt a little in that way when the king's scepter touched her," Rebecca wrote.

Hawthorne never came. The Civil War broke out; the railroad was cut; Virginia seceded. Wheeling became the center of pro-Union loyalties, soon the capital of self-proclaimed free New (later West) Virginia. Martial law was declared; the local theater turned into a jail; an island in the river, visible from Rebecca's window, a prison camp. The house directly across the street from the Harding's was commandeered for General Rosecrans' Union Army Western Department headquarters.

Rebecca's brother Dick, along with several other young men of the Harding circle, made plans to join the Secessionists. They were talked out of it only at the last minute by the mayor: "It would ruin their families . . . he spoke particularly of Pa," Rebecca wrote a cousin.

And in the midst of this, in mid-May, Fields sent back *A Story of Today*: "It assembles the gloom too depressingly."

Rebecca's letter reveals how shaken she was. She begged Fields to tell her "if that was the only objection, the one you assign?" She "thanked him for candor and kindness." She asked: "If you do not think I could alter the story, shall I try again, or do you care to have me as a contributor?"

He wrote back at once, assuring her that the *Atlantic* wanted very much to keep her—and suggesting that she dispel some of the gloom, then resubmit the book. Fearful lest he lose his great discovery, he asked his young wife, Annie, to write also—a letter of such strong intelligent admiration, it was the start of Rebecca's closest and most supporting literary friendship, though in this beginning, not necessarily in the right direction. "I will try to meet Mr. Fields' wishes of being more cheerful," Rebecca agreed, "though humor had need to be as high as God's sunshine to glow cheerily on Virginia soil just now."

What made her agree? Isolated, had she so little confidence in her own judgment? Was the terror of the oblivion from which she was just emerging so great, the need for the verification publication gives so compelling? Was she (a woman in that day) so afraid of jeopardizing the one way seemingly open to independence, occupation, esteem, self-worth?

At just this time, one of Rebecca's literary admirers, L. Clarke Davis, already a regular correspondent, wrote asking her to contribute to a new Philadelphia magazine, *Peterson's*, for which he was a reader. It would be a different kind of writing—entertainment not literature.

Perhaps *Life in the Iron Mills had* been a fluke, "the novelty of the scene," and not the achievement she had tried to make it, had believed it to be. Perhaps the merit of *A Story of Today* was self-delusion too, as was her being worthy of a place in the exalted *Atlantic* company. She promised to write for *Peterson's*.

For six weeks Rebecca struggled with the revision of *A Story of Today*. Without the original manuscript, there is no way of knowing what the gloom was that she dispelled, and how much was marred and lost thereby; how much of the imperfect working out of character, the marks of haste and of patching, are in the original, how much the result of shaken judgment in a revision having to be made, furthermore, under "the shadow of death," "from the border of the battlefield."

In the beginning, she defends the very concerns of the book:

> The shadow of death has fallen on us. . . . Do not call us traitors . . . who choose to be cool and silent through the fever of the hour,—who choose to search in common things for auguries . . . [who] hint that there are yet other characters besides that of Patriot in which a man may appear creditably. . . .
>
> I want you to go down into this common every-day drudgery . . . and consider if there might not be in it also a great warfare. . . . It has its slain. Men and women, lean-jawed, crippled in the slow, silent battle, are in your alleys.

Margret Howth has gone into a textile mill as a bookkeeper to "support a helpless father and mother; it was a common story." Holmes, the man she loves and who loves her, has broken off their secret engagement.

> He had turned his back on love and kindly happiness and warmth, on all that was weak and useless in the world . . . All men around him were doing the same,—thrusting and jostling and struggling up, up. It was the American motto, Go ahead; mothers taught it to their children; the whole system was a scale of glittering prizes. He at least saw the higher meaning of the truth.

He is "one of the new men who will mould the age." Knowles (not too successfully modeled after Doctor LeMoyne), Margret's employer and the mill owner, is in the process of selling his mill. "His veins thick with the blood of a despised race"—he is part Indian—"a disciple of Garrison, you know," he plans to use the money to organize in "the great city, with its stifling gambling-hells, its negro-pens, its foul cellars," and to make available a communal "new Arcadia." It is for this work he seeks Margret's help.

"You will fail, Knowles," predicts Margret's blind father (long-time adversary to Knowles, as Rebecca's father was to LeMoyne):

> ". . . any plan, Phalanstery or Community, call it what you please, founded on self-government, is based on . . . the tawdriest of shams. . . . There never was a thinner-crusted Devil's egg in the world than democracy. . . .
>
> "Any despotism is better than that of newly enfranchised serfs. . . . Your own phantom, your Republic, your experiment to prove that all men are born free and equal—what is it to-day?"

"Don't sneer at Knowles," the author says:

> Your own clear, tolerant brain, that reflects all men and creeds alike, like colorless water, drawing the truth from all, is very different, doubtless, from this narrow, solitary soul, who thought the world waited for him to fight down his one evil. . . . An intolerant fanatic, of course. But the truth he did know was so terribly real to him. . . . And then, fanatics must make history for conservative men to learn from, I suppose.

From Knowles, and from the black peddlar Lo with whom she feels the tie of identity, Margret glimpses and feels the "unhelped pain of life." During an early morning walk with Lo, memorable for the descriptive immediacy of the changing mists, the transition from the countryside's beauty into the city slums where Margret works, Lo, in the closeness of shared response, tells Margret of how her childhood in the mill deformed her:

> It was a good while I was there: from seven year old till sixteen. 'T seemed longer t' me 'n 't was. 'T seemed as if I'd been there allus,—jes' forever, yoh know, . . . like as I was part o' th' engines, somehow. Th' air used to be thick in my mouth, black wi' smoke 'n' wool 'n' smells.
>
> In them years I got dazed in my head, I think. 'T was th' air 'n' th' work. . . .'T got so that th' noise o' th' looms went on in my head night 'n' day,—allus thud, thud. 'N' hot days, when th' hands was chaffin' 'n' singin', th' black wheels 'n' rollers was alive, starin' down at me, 'n' th' shadders o' th' looms was like snakes creepin'.—creepin' anear all th' time.

As Margret and Knowles later walk the city, he looks

> about him as into a seething caldron, in which . . . the blood of uncounted races was fused . . . where creeds, philosophies, centuries old, grappled hand to hand in their death-struggle,—where innumerable aims and beliefs and powers of intellect, smothered rights and triumphant wrongs, warred together, struggling for victory.
>
> Vulgar American life? He thought it a life more potent, more tragic in its history and prophecy, than any that has gone before.

They go to a hovel, a temporary one-room refuge he has established,

> swarming with human life. Women, idle trampers, whiskey-bloated, filthy, lay half-asleep, or smoking, on

the floor. . . . Half-naked children crawled about in rags. . . . In the corner slept a heap of half-clothed blacks. Going on the underground railroad to Canada.

"Did I call it a bit of hell? [Knowles rages.] It's only a glimpse of the under-life of America,—God help us!—where all men are born free and equal. . . .

"And you," he said, savagely, "you sit by the road-side, with help in your hands, and Christ in your heart, and call your life lost, quarrel with your God, because that mass of selfishness has left you. . . . Look at these women. What is their loss, do you think? Go back, will you, and drone out your life whimpering over your lost dream, and go to Shakespeare for tragedy when you want it? Tragedy! Come here,—let me hear what you call this."

Lo, much mourned, dies from burns after a fire set in the mills by her father, who is hounded as an ex-con-vict. Knowles, an old man, has no money to finance his dreams.

The tacked-on happy ending is grotesquely evident, a contrived reformation, out of it true love triumphing: the success-is-all Holmes converts to plainer, older vir-tues; Margret, obeying "the law of her woman's nature," marries him and gives up working for social change. There is even an oil well opportunely gushing up in the back yard to keep them from poverty.

It is an awkward book, sometimes embarrassingly bad. Nevertheless, it is also a rewarding, fascinatingly native book of substance and power. It accomplishes much of what Rebecca set out to do in that first ardent fever of work after the *Atlantic*'s acceptance. Essential reading for any literary or social historian concerned with the period, *Margret Howth: A Story of Today* justifies re-evaluation, perhaps resurrection.

Fields had the revision back at the end of July and accepted it at once. Rebecca hastily concocted the promised mystery novel for *Peterson's*. Then she stopped writing.

She could no longer "search in common things for auguries." That "poor everyday warfare for bread" could not hold attention with the bloody, physical war all around. Wheeling was under threat of immediate attack from Lee's surrounding armies and in "a state of panic not to be described."

She had schooled herself to observe and read behaviors; now the behaviors were more than she could absorb. "Malignant personal hatreds wearing patriotic masks . . . a slavery of intolerance; hands wet with a brother's blood for Right"; fears, corruptions, political jobbery; the behavior of women—that she thought she understood:

> They had taken the war into their whole strength, like their sisters, North and South: as women greedily do anything that promises to be an outlet for what power of brain, heart, or animal fervor they have, over what is needed for wifehood or maternity.

If there were, as there must also have been, evidences of true conviction, nobility, they were obscured for her by the other behaviors, and by her inability to come to a whole-selfed stand on the war.

Southern bred, nearly all her blood ties were Secessionist in sympathy, when not in action. Her other bonds and allegiances were Northern. Slavery, the greatest of wrongs, must be ended. But the Federal government was making it clear that the war was not to end slavery, it was to end secession from the Union. Secession to her was a state's right, "though I never would, never could, live in a slave confederacy." Neither should slaves: the enslaved had an absolute right to their freedom. Yet how would they, who had never been permitted freedom, know how to use it? Deep in her was the Southern guilt-fear: freed slaves might take revenge. Justified retribution; the innocent would suffer as well, wrong again come out of right. Round and round within her, the doubt and fear and contradiction, while all about her was destruction and bloodletting, with slavery seemingly no closer to being ended.

*Margret Howth: A Story of Today* began appearing serially, the lead piece in the October 1861 *Atlantic*. Whether it was this evidence of herself as a writer that helped, or not, Rebecca returned to writing—the most chilling and perfectly executed of her stories, "John Lamar."[14]

Set in the West Virginia hills in icy November, where Secesh Bushwhacker atrocities have been followed by Union Snakehunter reprisals, John Lamar, a Georgian slaveowner, is being held captive by Union forces under the command of his closest friend since childhood, Captain Dorr. Lamar is planning escape, an escape completely dependent on his barefoot body slave, Ben, to whom the North secretly means freedom. ("At two, Ben, remember. We will be free to-night, old boy." It is typical of Lamar's obliviousness that he says "we" without irony.) Ben listens to the two friend-enemies, Lamar and Dorr, talk; first Dorr, then Lamar:

> "This slave question must be kept out of the war. It puts a false face on it.". . .
>
> "There is Ben. What, in God's name, will you do with him? Keep him a slave, and chatter about self-government? Pah! The country is paying in blood for the lie, to-day. . . ."
>
> . . . As for Ben, crouching there, if they talked of him like a clod, heedless [of his presence] . . . we all do the same, you know. . . .
>
> ". . . Let the white Georgian come out of his sloth, and the black will rise with him. . . .When we have our Lowell, our New York . . . when we stand where New England does, Ben's son will be ready for his freedom."

Ben concludes that North *or* South, the "kind" intention is the same: to keep him (and his) always in slavery. An hour before the planned escape, half frozen, "crushing down and out the old parasite affection for his master . . . [his] muddy blood heating, firing with the same heroic dream that bade Tell and Garibaldi lift up their hands to God, and cry aloud that they were men and free," Ben kills the sleeping Lamar, then turns south, not north—"he had a lost life to avenge," a "past of cruelty and oppression." The "canting abolitionist" Union soldier who had earlier called Ben "man and brother," and at a camp prayer meeting, while Ben listened, had preached the Lord's vengeance to the Babylon South—"As she hath done unto my people, be it done unto her"—is left to stand sentry over the dead man. "Humble, uncertain," the words he has said earlier reiterate themselves:

> The day of the Lord is nigh; it is at hand; and who can abide it?

*And who can abide it?*

FOR MONTHS, invitations had been coming from the North, some from fabled names. The Fields, who had invited her from the beginning, stepped up the frequency of their urgings. Now Rebecca was desperate to go.

It was not only the need to get away from the war. The old sense of constriction, of longing for more than her life was, had roused up, intensified by the constant presence of death. She wanted to be, for a while, with people to whom literature was life; she wanted responding flesh and blood confirmation of her reality as a thinking, writing being. Nothing in Wheeling, outside of herself, confirmed it. No one regarded her as the nation's most significant new writer whose work was of real importance. She was still just Harding's spinster daughter, devoted, quiet, queer in her unshared interests. Within her family, life went on as before— her writing fitted in, their needs prior. Proud as they probably were of the recognition given her, her subject matter may have precluded any discussion of it.

When her father became ill, a breakdown—"strain of the war"—it was taken for granted (most of all by herself) that she would put her writing aside, as if it were china painting, to devote herself to him. No one expected of her brothers that they should do the same. Across the street, to take over the Western Department, came General Frémont, the "Pathfinder." For a few hours now and then, when she could leave her father, she had occasional heady draughts, from Frémont, from his remarkable wife Jessie Benton, of what friends of range, culture, response, might mean to her. But the Frémonts were not to be in Wheeling long.[15]

Months before she had promised Annie Fields a photograph of herself. Now she had one taken, and a copy sent to her Philadelphia correspondent, Clarke Davis, as well. She was coming to count on his letters more and more in this drouth time.

The eyes look directly out of an ardent, compelling face, a strong intelligent face; the hair, carefully arranged, severely parted, falls in luxurious black curls onto plump beautiful shoulders that the dress is cut low enough to disclose. Was it at this time she copied out from Margaret Fuller:

> With the intellect I always have, always shall overcome: but that is not the half of the work. The life, the life, O my God shall the life never be sweet? Nature vindicates her right, and I feel all Italy glowing beneath the Saxon crust.[16]

Money was on her mind. For what? Family needs?

The journey? The simple freedom of being able for the first time in her life, without dependence, to buy something without asking, to give money away or save it? She asked Fields for the advance of $100 refused earlier for the book publication of *Margret Howth*. He sent $200, and as the book was doing well (2,500 copies in three editions), another $200. She scribbled some stories for *Peterson's*. That fitted in with her shredded time, as serious writing could not (and any one of them paid more than all of *Margret Howth* had brought her).

It was April, one year after publication of *Life in the Iron Mills*, before she could write Annie that yes, she *would* come North, "as soon as her father's health permitted." But still she could not go—the "minor trouble of an escort." No unmarried lady, not even a well-known author with earnings of her own to finance a journey, was free to travel by herself. "O Annie," she wrote her Boston friend, "how good it must be to be a man when you want to travel."[17]

In the uninterrupted hours that came sometimes now, free too of the worst of the weight of concern about her father, Rebecca returned to serious writing: another Civil War story, *David Gaunt*, published in 1862 in the *Atlantic*. The sense of torn loyalties, intermixed right-wrong, hands wet with a brother's blood for the Right, are in this too (a pacifist minister, after agonizing introspection—*must* murder be the way to justice, peace?—enlists in the war against slavery; is betrayed by his noble beliefs into killing his benefactor), but a love theme (she Confederate, he Northern, of course) twines mawkishly through it all, and there is a distraught, watery, hasty quality to the writing.

The distraught quality was not only in the story. Her schoolteacher brother, Wilson, needing to go to Boston anyway, had agreed to take her with him in early June. Now that the trip was definite, its terrors and temerities overcame her. In the long ordeal-hours sitting by her father, without the stay of her writing, it had come to seem odd and dreamlike that she was an established writer, let alone one thought fit to be invited into the most select of companies. In her was something of Hugh Wolfe's outsider feeling, of "a mysterious class that shone down with glamour of another order of being." She who was reticent, who had kept to herself, would be on display, expected to respond. She who was backwoods and self-taught and terribly conscious of the deficiencies of that; she who was lonely, opinionated, defiantly so if necessary (for that was the other side of her reticence, a tart outspokenness), was going into the Temple of Athens, where perhaps she had no right, no place, was an interloper. Frightening.

It was in this condition that she arrived at the Fields. She had come to the right house. Annie Fields, that great "angel in the house" of literature, was so excited by the prospect of having her admired Rebecca there that her joy was infectious. "You never knew, did you, Annie," Rebecca wrote later, "how downrightedly scared and lonesome I felt that night, and how your greeting took it all away." In the sun of this genuine love and delight in her company, Rebecca bloomed.

All through her Boston visit, she had the exhilarating experience of being her best self, without self-consciousness. No one seemed put off by directness, or participation, or interest, or seriousness. She was feted, dined, entertained, honored, *appreciated*, by the Brahmins, the *Atlantic* circle, the Areopagites. They found her intellectually impressive, witty, captivating; in one recorded instance, shockingly full blooded and direct, for she observed that *women feel physical desire for men, just as men do for women!*

Oliver Wendell Holmes, "the Autocrat [of the Breakfast Table], to whom the whole country was paying homage," was delighted to discover their mutual love for inscriptions in burying yards ("the strange bits of human history to be found or guessed at in them") and took a day off to show her his favorite gravestones in Mount Auburn cemetery.[18]

At an evening reception, Rebecca went over to talk with

> a tall, thin young woman standing alone in a corner. She was plainly dressed, and had that watchful, defiant air with which the woman whose youth is slipping away is apt to face the world which has offered no place to her.

She had wanted so much to meet her, she told Rebecca, that she had walked all the way home to Concord for her one decent dress. "'I'm very poor' . . . she had once taken a place as a 'second girl' [maid]." It was Louisa May Alcott.[19]

> Before I met her I had known many women and girls who were fighting with poverty and loneliness, wondering why God had sent them into a life where apparently there was no place for them. . . . soon after [she] wrote her "Hospital Sketches." Then she found her work and place in the world.

There were rich hours talking with Annie of books, of others, of themselves. Rebecca discovered that her friend, whose gifted, dedicated expenditure of self had already made the Fields' house a center of inspiration and hospitality for writers, herself hid a painfully shy need to write.[20]

Concord was a different experience. Some profound, unrecorded hurt which she never forgave occurred to Rebecca there. It never healed, indeed cankered with the years, and had serious consequences to her self, her attitudes, her writing. The nature of it is implied in the way she writes more than forty years later of Bronson Alcott and of Emerson, in her guarded (and not necessarily reliable) reminiscences, *Bits of Gossip*, published in 1904.

> . . . the first peculiarity which struck an outsider [was] . . . that while they thought they were guiding the real world, they stood quite outside of it, and never would see it as it was. . . . their views gave you the same sense of unreality, of having been taken, as Hawthorne said, at too long a range. . . . something was lacking,

some back-bone of fact. . . . To the eyes of an observer, belonging to the commonplace world, they . . . walked and talked . . . always apart from humanity.

She stayed with the Hawthornes at Wayside, Hawthorne who permitted almost no visitors now. "Here comes the Sage of Concord," Hawthorne told her at breakfast early her very first morning. "He [Alcott] is anxious to know what kind of human beings come up from the back hills in Virginia."

Emerson came shortly thereafter. Her tongue was "dry with awe" ("I went to Concord, a young woman from the backwoods, firm in the belief that Emerson was the first of living men"). It loosened, after listening the entire morning, along with Emerson and Hawthorne,[21] to Alcott's "orotund" sentences

paeans to the war, the "armed angel which was wakening the nation to a lofty life unknown before."

I had just come up from the border where I had seen the actual war; the filthy spewings of it; the political jobbery in Union and Confederate camps; the malignant personal hatreds wearing patriotic masks, and glutted by burning homes and outraged women, the chances in it, well improved on both sides, for brutish men to grow more brutish, and for honorable gentlemen to degenerate into thieves and sots. War may be an armed angel with a mission, but she has the personal habits of the slums.

Rebecca found herself tartly, though tremblingly, saying substantially the above.

> This would-be seer who was talking of it, and the real seer who listened, knew no more of war as it was, than I had done [as a child] in my cherry-tree when I dreamed of bannered legions of crusaders debouching in the misty fields.

Alcott's orotund sentences went right on, till Hawthorne "rose lazily to his feet, and said quietly: 'We cannot see that thing at so long a range. Let us go to dinner,' and Mr. Alcott suddenly checked the droning flow of his prophecy and quickly led the way to the dining-room."

Her dislike for Alcott, "the vague, would-be prophet," is unconcealed and sometimes vitriolic. She found Emerson's deep respect for him "almost painful to see."

For all Emerson's flattering and receptive attention to her, his "exquisite courtesy," she felt he regarded her not as Rebecca Harding, writer, human being, but as some kind of specimen.

> He studied souls as a philologist does words, or an entomologist beetles. He approached each man with bent head and eager eyes. "What new thing shall I find here?" . . . He took from each man his drop of stored honey, and after that the man counted for no more to him than any other robbed bee.

Hawthorne, by contrast, was the Boston feeling all over again, vivified by the happiness and sense of privilege of being near the revered writer who meant so much to her.

There was one awkward evening though. Elizabeth Peabody, Hawthorne's sister-in-law, seized the presence of the celebrated, mysterious author of *Life in the Iron Mills* as an occasion for a surprise party. "They've been here [back from Europe] two years," she told Rebecca, as townspeople filtered in,

> and nobody has met Mr. Hawthorne. People talk. It's ridiculous! There's no reason why Sophia should not go into society. So I just made an excuse of your visit to bring them in.

Hawthorne's wife rescued him; he was permitted to escape. Rebecca understood, approved—but "I have not yet quite forgiven [Miss Elizabeth] the misery of that moment."

The next morning Hawthorne took Rebecca for a long walk; made a special point of showing her the Old Manse where he had lived when he first married; and then, perhaps at her request, they wandered through Sleepy Hollow cemetery. He was in high spirits. "Yes," he said, surveying the surroundings, the hills and river below, "we New Englanders begin to enjoy ourselves—when we are dead."

They sat a long while in the deep grass and quiet beauty, the sense of communion strong between them. It was that bad time in Hawthorne's life Van Wyck Brooks describes so affectingly:

> He had wasted away . . . and, hard as he tried to write, pulling down the blinds and locking his door, he could not bring his mind into focus. The novel became two

novels, and the two became four. . . . [All] drifted in confusion through his mind, their outlines melting into one another. Even his theme eluded him . . . until he could scarcely bear to touch his blurred and meaningless manuscripts.[22]

What kinship did he feel with this young writer beside him, for whom he had broken his seclusion? He had written greatly of the unpardonable sin, of irremediable evil within. She had written—in one instance close to greatly—of another kind of unpardonable sin, of an evil she believed remediable. He was near the close of his work.[23] Her literary life was at the beginning. Or so it seemed.

> As we walked back, the mists gathered and the day darkened overhead. Hawthorne . . . grew suddenly silent, and before we reached home the cloud had settled down again upon him, and his steps lagged heavily.
>
> I left Concord that evening and never saw him again. He said good-by, hesitated shyly, and then, holding out his hand, said:—"I am sorry you are going away. It seems as if we had known you always."

With that accolade, she turned toward home.

There was a stop in New York, where she stayed with the Frémonts. One Sunday she sat in an immense audience as an invited guest at Plymouth Church, where the most unusual of the tributes to her was paid. Henry Ward Beecher, that "huge, lumbering man," foremost preacher of his day, had sat next to her at a dinner party, had listened to her tell of and sing certain old forgotten backwoods hymns. That morning, in her honor, the congregation sang, one by one, all of those hymns. "I shall never forget that morning."

In Philadelphia, the personal (and secret) reason for the journey from home waited: L. Clarke Davis. Their correspondence, begun with his admiration for *Life in the Iron Mills* a year ago, continuing with the request that she become a contributor to *Peterson's*, had deepened into intimacy—on his side, into courtship. He was attracted by what would have made most men shun her: her very achievement, seriousness, power; her directness and sardonic eye for sham; the evidence of a rich secret life.

He, like her, was schooled in protective reticence. Freed in letters from the self-consciousness of outside selves, social situations, the dialogue of bodies, they came to know each other in a way that their actual presence might have precluded. Now they wanted the presence.

They were delighted by what they found. He liked her reticence with others. He liked her unvarnished, outspoken, intense. He liked her physically. It was reciprocal. By the time the week was over, they had agreed to marry.

There is no record of when she told her family. For thirty-one years (except for those unknowns out of whom she wrote Lo, Hugh Wolfe, Holmes), they had been her emotional life. In the last years she had come closer and closer to her solitary, austere father. Bound to them as deeply as she was, she could not help but care what their reaction would be.

At that time, a woman who had not married by the age of thirty-one had long ago ceased to be thought of as marriageable. There would be the flavor of something unnatural, vaguely shameful about it happening now. To Rebecca's father, not yet completely recovered, the impending loss might be considered betrayal—so dependent had he become on her devotion and companionship. And both parents would naturally feel concern about the nature of the match.

Clarke Davis was four years younger than Rebecca, without established situation or income. He had to work on various additional jobs (editing legal periodicals, reading for *Peterson's*) to support himself while he clerked in a law office, preparing for the bar. How then could he responsibly marry? Furthermore, he was a declared abolitionist, and radical.

The family secreted the knowledge among themselves. No public announcement of the betrothal was made. But Rebecca must have made her determination to marry Davis clear: it was understood that the marriage *would* eventually take place.

Home again, Rebecca sat down almost at once to write—not romance, not another Civil War story (though the war was as agonizing to her as ever)[24]— but out of the center from which *Life in the Iron Mills* came. An almost unendurable account of the misuse, the refusal of development to a blind slave child, a musical genius, "Blind Tom." It appeared in the *Atlantic* in November 1862.

*Was* there a Blind Tom? A "coal-black" child "of the lowest negro type, from which only field-hands can be made," who never received instruction yet could reproduce on the piano any music heard once ("intricate symphonies," Beethoven, Mendelsohn, "intact in brilliancy and symmetry"); who, left to himself, composed "unknown, wild . . . harmonies which he had never heard, had learned from no man. . . . Never glad . . . one inarticulate, unanswered question of pain in all."

*Was* he paraded before audiences ("a more fruitful source of revenue than tobacco-fields"), subjected to exhausting tests, exhibited at the White House ("Being a slave . . . never was taken into a Free State; for the same reason his master refused advantageous offers from European managers.")? And

> that feature of the concerts which was the most painful . . . the moments when his master was talking [to the audience], and Tom was left to himself,—when a weary despair seemed to settle on the distorted face and the stubby little black fingers, wandering over the keys, spoke for Tom's own caged soul within. . . . all the pain and pathos of the world [in it].

Was it so? Or is this fiction, the kind of fiction that is truth for the tearing possibility in it?

"You cannot help Tom, either," she ends, addressing the North directly, revealing her consciousness of more than parlors during her stay there:

> He was in Richmond in May. But (do you hate the moral to a story?) in your own kitchen, in your own back-alley, there are spirits as beautiful, caged in forms

as bestial, that you *could* set free, if you pleased. . . .
they are more to be pitied than Tom,—for they are
dumb.

Whatever transport there was in the writing of it,
the small payment the *Atlantic* made was shock into a
different reality. She set herself to concoct a serial, *The
Second Life*, for *Peterson's*, and wrote to Fields, appealing
to him to make such writing unnecessary. Even anonymously, she told him, she did not want to write the
thrillers, Gothics, mysteries, plot romances suitable for
*Peterson's*. She wanted to write only her best, for dis-
criminating *Atlantic* audiences. But *Peterson's* was now
paying $300 and more a story, $1,000 and more for
serials.[25]

> As times are, I am not justified in refusing the higher
> prices . . . I thought that I could say to you as a friend
> . . . that I hope Mr. Ticknor and you will give as much
> for future articles as you can legitimately afford.

She did not explain that "as times are" had to do
with the economic necessities of a forthcoming marriage: hers. It was not until January, half a year after the
betrothal, that the Fields were told in a letter to Annie,
her closest (and only) woman friend:

> It isn't easy for me to tell you this I don't know why.
> But you who are so happy in your married life will
> know how to ask for a blessing on mine. I *want* to tell
> you . . . of some one else, but it is harder than even
> to talk about myself. When you know him you won't

think much of *me*, in comparison. . . . Our marriage was to have been the first of the winter, but I had to defer it [because of family illness] until March the 5th, and . . . it will be strictly private. . . . Will you please . . . not to speak of this to anyone? No one here knows it except ourselves. . . . I never told you what my name would be—Davis. But I never *had* such trouble to write a letter before. O Annie, my summer days are coming now.

*My summer days are coming now.*

All that had been impressed on her from babyhood impelled her to the believing of it. "Love and marriage—a woman's fulfillment." "When you loved, you fulfilled the law of your woman's nature." You were no longer of those whom "God had thought unworthy of every woman's right, to love and be loved."

All that was passionate and loving and had had to be denied in her nature, never doubted it. "Nature vindicates her right, and I feel all Italy glowing beneath the Saxon crust." "The *natural* need to love and be loved." Nature, God, Right; Need, Law, Fulfillment.

And yet, and yet:

Rebecca, writer, thirty-two, had known another kind of summer days, fulfilling another need and law of her nature, vindicating another kind of a right. Where was *their* place to be?

In "Paul Blecker,"[26] a mawkish story begun about the time of her letter to Annie, there is a girl (not otherwise like Rebecca), wanting marriage, children, *and* to use her "dumb power" in men's world of achievement.

She "is perpetually self-analyzing—in a hysteric cling-ing, embracing the chimera of the Women's Rights prophets with her brain, and thrusting it aside with her heart." But heart and brain are not separates. To attain the health of happiness, they must find harmony—not be split in a war within the being that must contain them both. Chimera is a monster only in myth; in actu-ality, it is a whole organism containing both female and male.

Harmony or war? Myth or reality? The needs and laws of nature? *What would happen now?*

REBECCA HARDING, thirty-two, and Clarke Davis, twenty-eight, were married on March 5, 1863, in Wheeling. Only her family was present. No honey-moon. They went directly to Philadelphia, to the home of Clarke's sister Carrie, where for the next fourteen months they were to live. It was a house crowded with children; meals and housekeeping had to be shared; Carrie was often ill, and always (it was her house) present.

Even more than Clarke, Rebecca came to marriage with strongly established patterns of living, including the practice of solitude. Now neither had even the physical space of a room of one's own. The most inti-mate and tasking of relationships had to seek a tena-ble way to live in the midst of the clamor of everyday unavoidable relationship with others—necessitating (Rebecca would feel it most) constant consciousness and consideration for them.

In Wheeling, years of close living had bought the safety of unspoken understanding; knowledge of limits, one's own and others'; what to accept, resist, avoid; what one spoke of, what was best kept silent. Here it was all to learn.

Rebecca's first venture was to the Philadelphia public library—at last she lived somewhere where there was a circulating library, and a great one. She used her status as a leading *Atlantic* writer to secure reserved desk space, as well as a card.

Annie Fields came down for a flying one-day visit. Concealing any dismay she may have felt at the newlyweds' circumstances, she set about arranging a series of visits and invitations from distinguished Philadelphians. She knew in Rebecca the longing "for music, art, the companionship of thinkers, scholars." Lucretia Mott, the great, long-time abolitionist and women's rights leader, came to call. Rebecca loved her, "a little vivid delicate creature, alive with magnetic power . . . no man had a more vigorous brain or ready eloquence."27 But she evaded further relationship with other Philadelphians, the "ponderous matrons whose turrets of white hair atop symbolize a sort of social Gibraltar"; and even those with whom Annie had hoped she and Clarke would find mutuality were dismissed by Rebecca (the shadow of Concord?) as "philanthropists, litterateurs, people with missions."

The avoidance may have been partly self-protective: they had no home in which to entertain reciprocally; the position of husband to a famous wife was not easy for an as yet unestablished man; Clarke's likings for people had to be considered; and there was the problem of Rebecca's time and energies, seemingly less and less hers than ever.

LETTERS FROM Wheeling kept telling her how frail and lonesome her father was. Clarke, increasingly obsessed with the (mis)conduct of the war, seemed to speak of nothing else; passionately involved himself in organizing abolitionist meetings against Lincoln's expediency. Rebecca reminded him that it was God who had the war in His hand, and not he, but to little effect. She wrote the story of "Ellen" who wandered freely, but it was not *Atlantic* quality. She had to send it to *Peterson's*. Carrie was ill, recovered, was ill again. There were always children, and things that needed doing, and then redoing. Clarke and she never seemed to be alone when he was home—and the walls were so thin. "If any individual live too much in relations, so that he becomes a stranger to the resources of his own nature, he falls, after a while, into a distraction, or imbecility. . . ."[28] The library hours and distance were not really convenient. Clarke kept smoking all those cigars, though she tried to help him cut down by offering him ice cream, and then having to eat half herself. Carrie was sick. It looked as if Clarke would enlist, or let himself be drafted. It was five months and she was not writing at all. Her father was worse. There were always children and a lot of things that needed redoing.

Then, in late July, she did the only thing. She fell

into a distraction, or imbecility, an "undefined illness" (brain fever and nervous prostration are hinted at) that in our day we call a breakdown. Immediately she had freedom from household tasks, idleness, isolation, care, indulgence, removal, release to herself.

Although she probably did not know it yet, she was also pregnant.

Late in September, she could write a note to Annie. Without specifying why she had needed treatment, she told her abruptly that allopathy and homeopathy had been useless, and now "finally desperately" she had "gone back to [her] old Western habit [her girlhood habit] of walking" walking walking to exhaustion. Philadelphia streets, not Wheeling's. Now she was better: "I'm so glad, for I didn't know how to be sick."

The "better" was premature. Late in October, there is another letter:

My dear *dear* Annie: I wanted to write before only to say I love you. God knows how dear and tender all love has grown to me now, but at first I was not able and now the doctor forbids the least reading or writing for fear of bringing back the trouble in my head. Ma is with me. Clarke has been waiting every day to have some good news to send you, to write. Sometimes I wish the time would be longer. I don't know—these days have been so like the valley of the shadow of death that I grow afraid of the end. . . . I wish you would pray for us.

I must tell you one happy thing. If I get well we are going directly to live by ourselves—it is all clear now. *You* know all that means to me.

Her mother brought her to Wheeling to convalesce. She wrote she was thinking of composing a Christmas story, forgetting that it was far too late for any publication. Sometime in November she went back to Philadelphia:

> It was such a happy homecoming, but I was still weak enough to feel my heart beat and the tears come at a little petting, and they did pet me. . . . How dear you are to me, Annie. I never felt before how hard it was to justify my right to love as since I was sick. . . . Sometimes I have a horror, Annie, that it will all disappear like a dream, that I will become suddenly indifferent to you all—I am foolish to speak in this way, but I cannot help it.

She returned for Christmas to her family in Wheeling, sending Annie a mysterious note the night before going:

> I have had much to think of and to feel—for others, not myself. I could tell you a story which I cannot write, sadder and stranger than any fiction, which has made the days and nights very feverish for a long time. Someday I will tell you but maybe now, I ought not to have even said this much.
>
> There's a happy ending coming at last, I hope.

The first hint to Annie of the coming baby.

"It was not a very merry Christmas. Father is not dangerously ill," she wrote Annie, "but enough to make him nervous and even morbid in his desire to have me with him." The good-bys were agonizing, the more so for the constraint.

After Rebecca came home, rearrangements in their living situation were made. She had some space and time. All January, February, March, the six-seven-eight-month pregnant Rebecca wrote and re-wrote a story which the July 1864 *Atlantic* featured as its lead piece.[29] It deserved that honor, and perhaps a more permanent one.

"The Wife's Story" is about a "terror and temptation which had beset" a married life from the beginning, and is now taking "a definite shape and hold." The wife had married fifteen months before into a ready-made family (five children and a ward) whose habits and temperaments are alien to her. Economic disaster has come to them; they face "the coarse struggle . . . for bread and butter." The temptation is a life in art; the terror is in considering it, for it might mean giving up human love, hurting and abandoning those who need her. She yields—to discover that the talent itself is mediocre, a delusion; the world in which it has to function, commercial and degrading; and the end result is shame, death to her loved husband, the fate of a social outcast for herself.

But wait: it is all in the fantasies of a brain-fever dream; it never happened. The wife wakes from the nightmare illness "thirsty for love, and to love," and safe: babe at her breast, husband at her side, loved ones surrounding her. An example, furthermore, for the young ward:

. . . mother, here, will tell you a woman has no better

work in life than the one she has taken up: to make herself a visible Providence to her husband and child.

Happy conclusion, and satisfyingly reassuring to the prevalent attitudes of her readers. But there is anguish in the story. It is there in the extremity of Hetty's punishment had she acted—self-deluded fool, death-causer, outcast; it is there in the torment of Hetty's situation, which Rebecca makes so actual. (And it is implicit in the choice of endings: even 108 years ago, there were a handful of women with family who had demonstrated that in exceptional instances, for a few, a third ending was possible.)

Aside from any light or dark that it casts on factors in Rebecca's breakdown, "The Wife's Story" is important (and fascinating) for the detailing of this anguish, the working of woman's conflict between commitment to other human beings and the need to carry on serious work. The literature of this anguish is sparse.[30] "The Wife's Story" is the first, and still among the most revealing:

> I was so hungry for affection that night! I would have clung to a dog that had been kind to me. . . . The motherless boy, holding himself up by my knees, was more sturdy than I that night and self-reliant: never could have known, in his most helpless baby-days, the need with which I, an adult woman, craved a cheering word, and a little petting.

This immediately after she has acceded for the first time to the "temptation." Each succeeding concern with her art is followed by such a craving for love, for tenderness; an intensified sensitivity to her husband's admirable qualities; a rousing of physical desire at the touch or look of him. And this in turn is followed by resentment of what she makes herself scorn as "weak fever of the flesh"; or by a devaluation of her husband and their relationship; or by a re-dwelling on her work, and her circumstances that deny it.

In a long passage, Hetty tries to "judge" the days of her married life:

> . . . other years of my life thrust them aside, per-sistently, as foreign, alien to me. These others were to me home,—the thoughts that had held me nearest the divine life. . . . "The only object in life is to grow." . . . Margaret Fuller's motto. . . . There had been a time when I had dreamed of attaining Margaret's stature; and as I thought of that, some old subtile flame stirred in me with a keen delight. New to me, almost; for, since my baby was born, my soul as well as my body had been weak and nauseated. . . . I had intended my child should be reared in New England: what I had lacked in gifts and opportunities he should pos-sess. . . . But the child was a girl,[31] a weazen-faced little mortal, crying night and day like any other ani-mal. It was an animal, wearing out in me the strength needed by-and-by for its mental training. I sent it to a nurse in the country. . . . For days after that he [her father] looked paler, and his face had a quiet, settled look, as if he had tested the world and was done with it. . . . I do not remember that after this he ever called me Hetty. But he was cheerful as ever with the boys.

"Some latent, unconscious jar of thought" brings her

back to a time when she saw Rosa Bonheur's famous painting, "Horse-Fair":[32]

I remembered how some one had quoted her as saying, "Any woman can be a wife or mother, but this is my work alone."

I, too, had my gift: but one. But again the quick shiver of ecstasy ran through me;—it was my power, my wand with which to touch the world, my *"Vollmachtsbrief zum Glücke"*: was I to give it unused back to God? I could sing: not that only; I could compose music,—the highest soul-utterance. . . . I *had* been called, then,—set apart to a mission . . . and I had thrust it all aside—for what? A mess of weakest pottage,—a little love, silly rides behind Tinker, petting and paltering such as other women's souls grew imbecile without. It was the consciousness of this that had grown slowly on me in the year just gone; I had put my husband from me day by day because of it. . . . I could look now at my husband, and see the naked truth about us both. Two middle-aged people with inharmonious intellects: tastes and habits jarring at every step, clenched together only by faith in a vague whim or fever of the blood called love. Better apart: we were too old for fevers. If I remained with Doctor Manning, my role was outlined plain to the end: years of cooking, stitching, scraping together of cents: it was the fate of thousands of married women without means. . . . Better apart.

As I thought that, he laid Teddy [the small boy] down, and came towards me,—the usual uncertain, anxious half-smile on his face with which he regarded me. . . .

. . . he . . . put his hard hand gently on my shoulder. It made me turn faint, with some weakness that must have come down to me from my infant days. . . . I caught the sleeve of his dressing-gown in my fingers, and began smoothing it. It was the first thing I had ever made for him. I remembered how proud I was the evening he put it on.

"I was sure the life meant so much more to you than food or raiment," her husband says to her.

"What do you mean by the life? Have I found it here, Daniel?"
"No, Hester?"
"I want work fit for me," I said, almost fiercely. "God made me for a good, high purpose."
"I know," cheerfully. "We'll find it, dear: no man's work is kept back from him. We'll find it together."
But under the cheerfulness there was a sad quiet, as of one who has lost something forever, and tries to hide the loss from himself.

The intensified sensitivity to his pain overwhelms her. She caresses him:

"Why, why, child!"
"Call me Hetty, Daniel, I'd like to think that name belonged to me yet."

She gets up, brings him his slippers, kneels to put them on:

Another of the old foolish tricks gone long ago. There was a look on his face which had not been there this many a day. He had such a credulous heart, so easy to waken into happiness. I took his wrist in my bony hands, to raise myself; the muscles were like steel, the cording veins throbbing with health; there was an indescribable rest in the touch.

"Daniel," I said, looking him full in the face, "I'd like to have no mission in God's world. I'd like to give up my soul, and forget everything but you."

"Yes," she says later, "It's a fever . . . In the blood."

Each hardening of determination comes out of situations of drudgery ("Was [it] for this in reality God had made me?"), or out of reinvolvement with her music,

> the work of my life. . . . I got it [the score of an opera] out now by stealth, at night, putting my pen to it here and there, with the controlled fever with which a man might lay his hand on a dear dead face, if he knew the touch would bring it back to life. Was there any waking that dead life of mine?

Her final decision—to accept an offer for her opera to be produced, and to sing in it herself—is made as she sits mending the weekly heap of boys' half-washed, leather-stained socks after a long exhausting day of making-do:

> The actual dignity and beauty of [this family] life, God's truth itself, may have grown dim to me, behind a faint body and tired fingers; but let the hard-worked woman who is without that sin throw the first stone at me.

Each hardening is followed by acts of love, renewal of responsibility; magnified sensitivity to others' feelings; and terrible longing not to have the conflict.

To nestle down into this man's heart and life. To make his last years that warm Indian-summer day! I could do it! I! What utter rest there were in that!

Yet was this power within me to rot and waste?

The movement of the story is that of *David Gaunt*: the back and forth embracing of the chimera with her brain, and the thrusting it aside with her heart—until the resolution.

THE HAPPY ENDING is what Rebecca, big with child, must have believed those last few months, sitting beside a bleak stove thinking of "the great talking fires at home." She wrote to Annie:

> The air is warmer and the sunshine clearer. We read and walk and I sew a little. . . . The time has been full of a deep breath of content and waiting.
>
> All good things lie in the future.

Richard Harding Davis was born on April 18, 1864. He was named after Rebecca's father, whose death three weeks before had been kept secret from her until her mother could come and tell her. The telling coincided with the onset of labor. For a month she was very ill, kept to her bed. When Annie wanted to come and visit, Rebecca asked her not to until she was stronger and the baby had had "a chance to grow fat and better pleased with the new world he has found. Just now he is the smallest tiredest little thing, and homely too, only with big dark eyes."

Clarke found a cheap rooming house in Point Pleasant near the sea for the summer, and in fall they moved at last from Carrie's into a place by themselves—a rented yardless Philadelphia row house, "not a scrap of growing green anywhere in sight," one of several hundred others for streets around exactly like it. They christened it "Centre of the Universe," a name to be attached to wherever they lived.

In December she took her baby to Wheeling, where Clarke—building a law practice, immersed in political activities, editing, and working at the post office part-time—wrote her: "Dearest Pet, will you help your old Boy a little" with some writing?

Rebecca helped her "old Boy" and herself a lot those next months. Five *Atlantic* stories, and *Haunted Manor House*, a book-length mystery for *Peterson's*: writing very fast and from the surface, nothing she really cared about, not stopping to rewrite or revise. She wanted help in the house and a yard and vista and to live by the sea that in the one summer she had come so dearly to love.

She got help with the baby and another summer by the sea. She was pregnant again, and after a while the writing raveled off. It was just as well; in that seaside time she was dreaming up a new book. It would be a major work. She would write it carefully, take her time, not as with those potboilers she had spun off.

Charles Belmont was born in January 1866. It was nearly a year before Rebecca got to her book. In a cooped-up winter and spring, the babies, then Clarke, were sick. She wrote about Holmes again, his disillusionment with Rapp's Harmonist commune (an actual commune) in Pennsylvania. That was a lead piece in the *Atlantic* too, (in May 1866), her last. The money managed Point Pleasant for a third vivifying summer, and in the fall, with the noises of new neighbors from the adjoining houses in her ears (Clarke had moved them to another row house without telling her) and her toddlers in healthy voice, Rebecca started her planned major novel.

Her intention was to "publish it in book form, after giving it care and time," but as usual there were money problems. An offer from a new magazine, *Galaxy*, to serialize it was too tempting: she earned $3,600 for the serial rights alone.

From the beginning, the situation was nightmarish. Often there were only exhausted tag-ends of herself in tag-ends of time leftover after the house, Clarke, the babies, for a book that demanded all her powers, all her concentration. Sometimes she had to send off great chunks, unread, unworked, to meet the inexorable monthly deadline.

Editorial problems developed; but the pages poured on and on—868 printed pages.[33]

*Waiting for the Verdict*, finished in 1868, was intended to pose what Rebecca considered the basic question of the time: how was the nation going to redress the wrong of slavery? Were the freed slaves to have work, education, respect, freedom? The blacks, the nation, the future, were waiting for the verdict.[34]

Her black characters would show the full human spectrum, the "as they might be"; her white characters would show the reasons for hope—and for hopelessness. The best and worst of the South would be juxtaposed with what was best and worst in the North.

The Civil War is still going on. Nathan (Nat), a slave, makes his hazardous escape to freedom, involving many black and white lives with his own, learning all the way, and instructing others by example and words.[35] Unprepossessing outwardly and in his own esteem, with surface slave manners, he is a mover, deep observer, prophet, resourceful hero, whose dedication to freedom, opportunity, for his people is unshakable.

A Randolph of Virginia falls in love with Rosslyn, a Northern girl, for qualities the Southern belles do not possess. She converts him to her Northern practices of "democracy and energy and practicality and opening fields of work . . . where help is needed." He accepts her background: abolitionist, working class—"the class which you place on a par with your slaves"—even the secret of her birth: she is illegitimate.

His cousin, Margaret, also a Randolph though raised in the North,[36] is wooed and won by a brooding, immensely cultured, eminent Philadelphia surgeon, Dr. Broderip, who has cured her father. The doctor too has a birth secret—he is part black. Strongly affected by Nat—who turns out to be his half brother, not seen since early childhood—and through Nat by a new sense of the black situation, Dr. Broderip tells his fiancée *his* birth secret. "The negro blood is abhorrent" to her. She lets the truth about him be known. He is excluded from his hospital, spurned by his patients, and ostracized by "polite society." "The knowledge and skill acquired in all those patient years lay dead weight in his hands to-day." Margaret's Northern father, however, not only keeps his door open to the doctor, but organizes patients to fight for Broderip's right to continue practicing.

Nat slowly and successfully convinces Broderip that his place is helping to organize and lead a regiment of freed slaves:

> ". . . dey don't know who to trust. Dey hears dat de Yankees 'll sell dem down inter Cuba, an' as fur dere ole marsters—well, dey knows dem. . . . Dey'd fight like debbils under a man ob dere own cullor. . . . Dey calls M's Linkum Moses. Moses warn't a white man, an' a stranger," deliberately. "He wur a chile ob de slave woman, an' he went an' stole all de learnin' ob his masters, an' den come back an' took his people cross de riber inter freedom. *His own people*, suh."

Broderip is killed in action. There are numerous other characters and situations: battle, escape, plantation, army, hospital, street scenes; life-going-on-as-usual social scenes; bigotry, apathy, humanity, degrees of hypocrisy; action, suspense, talk, talk, talk—intense debate, "warring creeds," dissensions; confusion, contradictions, terror. There are surprising depths in the development of the main characters, most in Nat, Rosslyn, and the unprecedented, complex Dr. Broderip, torn between his whiteness and blackness. There is stereotype, slush, excess, caricature, melodrama, and occasional racism on Rebecca's part.

*Waiting for the Verdict* never became a great book. More than anyone else, Rebecca knew that she had failed. She had conceived, intended to write, a great novel. She had failed to write it; had not given (had) the self and time (or always the knowledge) to write it. "A great hope fell, you heard no noise, the ruin was within." She never attempted an ambitious book again.

She also knew that *Waiting for the Verdict* was a book of far more substance and compass than anything else being written—and praised—at the time; and that it alone recorded, tried to make sense of, the seething currents of the Civil War period. Partly because of the unselected unwieldiness, the first-draft character of some of the pages, partly because of disturbing truths and portents in the book, understandings far ahead of the time, almost no one recognized this.

"Sentimental propaganda for the negro dictates *Waiting for the Verdict*" is how one reviewer dismissed it. The kindest remark *The Nation* made in a lengthy three-column review on November 21, 1867, was that:

> As it stands, it preserves a certain American flavor. The author has evidently seen something corresponding to a portion of what she describes, and she has disengaged herself to a much greater degree than many of the female story-tellers of our native country from heterogeneous reminiscences of English novels.

Then it went on to say:

> Mrs. Davis has written a number of short stories, chiefly of country life in Virginia and Pennsylvania, all distinguished by a certain severe and uncultured strength, but all disfigured by an injudicious straining after realistic effects which leave nature and reality at an infinite distance behind and beside them. The author has made herself the poet of poor people— laborers, farmers, mechanics, and factory hands. She has attempted to reproduce in dramatic form their manners and habits and woes and wants. The intention has always been good, but the execution has, to our mind, always been monstrous. . . . She drenches the whole field beforehand with a flood of lachrymose sentimentalism, and riots in the murky vapors which rise. . . . It is enough to make one forswear for ever all decent reflection and honest compassion, and take refuge in cynical jollity and elegant pococurantism.

Pococurantism. I looked it up. It means caring little, being indifferent, nonchalant.

> . . . nothing is left but a crowd of ghastly, frowning, grinning automatons. The reader, exhausted by the constant strain upon his moral sensibilities, cries aloud for the good, graceful old nullities of the "fashionable novel."

It was about this time that Rebecca began her practice of ignoring reviews.[37] Primarily though, this was part of her rapid process of devaluing herself as a writer aspiring to art.

Never mind. She was at a time when she could say (indeed *had* to say, for it was true): "That is not all there is to life." The almost total immersion that comes to a woman in a culture where full responsibility for home and growing new lives are hers had engulfed Rebecca. The immediacy of Clarke, the house, two little ones at their most demanding, absorbing, alluring, "each day a new discovery in the unfolding miracle of human life," left little over for other intensities. She began keeping a diary—a wife and mother diary, not a writer's diary—wishing she

> could put in words the happy sense of home and love that is under and over all, the thousand little ways in which my Darling shows how strong and tender is his love, Harding's funny antics, the look of Charley's earnest blue eyes.

She went on writing, of course, contracting for a serial (after having said she never would again) for *Lippincott's*. No ambitious compass this time: this was going to be manageable, though still about something. The monthly deadlines once more proved "a tax on one's endurance. And the horror of being sick," or the children being sick, or of any of the other pulls and claims on her time.

*The Nation* reviewer, on October 22, 1868, approved of this book, *Dallas Galbraith*.

> In the conception and arrangement of her story, . . . [the author] displays no inconsiderable energy and skill. She has evidently done her best to make it interesting, and to give her reader, in vulgar parlance, his money's worth. . . .
> Mrs. Davis, in her way, is an artist.

Mrs. Davis having intended to be, and for a while having practiced being, an artist, had no such illusions. Mrs. Davis, in her way, was a professional workhorse in the field of letters for income, doing the best she could. Her writing had bought an end to the old economic terrors, and to drudgery; it had bought servant help and summers by the sea. It had also bought the need to keep writing—for money. She was writing articles and comments on the times now, as well as fiction. She added children's stories—highly moral—for *Youth's Companion*. She joined the staff of the New York *Tribune* as contributing editor and began a long stream of articles and editorials. Clarke became an editor too—for the Philadelphia *Inquirer*—and forgot about a law practice.

Home almost always, Rebecca longed more and more for sky, vista, sea, another view than brick. She was "making fresh attacks on Papa to move out of town," she wrote Annie, "but Papa reads his paper and won't hear."

With Rebecca's earnings, Papa in 1870 bought their permanent home. In Philadelphia. Another row house flanked for blocks around by identical twins—but impressive three-story brick ones this time, with yards.

If Rebecca looked out her window, for the rest of her life (except for the sea summers) it was to be this sliver of sky and those brick houses endlessly repeating themselves. No river, no hills, no slow stream of human life moving by on its way to and from work in the mills.

Her commonplace, the "Centre of the Universe," was suburban domestic now. She records a typical day:

The boys' bed is close by ours and at daylight they are awake. Charley generally asserting that he is "chivering cold" until he is taken into my arms. Then dear old Hardy puts his head up on the pillow and we whisper a while till the light in the transom shows that Annie is ready to dress. Then I get up and we have breakfast. Clarke rises at 9 or 10. After he has his breakfast he reads the *Inquirer*, smokes his pipe, and goes [to work]. . . . When he comes home he has a supper of raw oysters with me and a cup of tea and then to bed.

Up two or three hours before Clarke was, and until 10 or 11 at night when he came home, Rebecca was running the house, seeing to the things that had to be done or doing them herself; mothering, teaching, when necessary nursing the boys; evading the neighbors ("Love thy neighbor? . . . The well to do, fat person across the way? I hate my kind when they come within meddling distance")—and getting her writing done.

That first year in the new house, she collected some articles written in the high-tide time of "happy sense of home and love," wrote a few more, and published *Pro Aris et Focis* (For Altar and Hearth), a small book all for domesticity, motherhood—and against women's rights.

What were these "voices . . . high shrill and occasionally discordant" going on so about women's rights?

Equality? Women should no more feel inferior because they are not fit for men's work than men feel inferior because they are not fit for women's work.

Professions for women?

Some of that surplus female population who have no chance of rest[38] in a husband's house and many of whom unhappily have no provision for the actual wants of life

should have public occupations open to them; but not potential wives and mothers. Was it more a woman's work "to dissect babies rather than to suckle them"? And woman's brain,

being like the rest of her frame, of more delicate organization, is not capable of such sustained and continuous mental exertion as man's.

Women vote? Most were properly far too occupied with home responsibilities even to consider taking that on; the rest, the idle, vain, rich, were interested only in fashion and amusement. Besides, husbands did not *want* their wives in the coarse political arena; and wives would not go against their husband's wishes. Nor should. The Bible was clear on the matter: wives must obey their husbands. "If you do not wish to obey, do not marry."

Had Rebecca joined that succession of professional women (they are still with us today) who discourse— profitably—to other women on the ordained rightness, naturalness, and glories of keeping to woman's sphere, while themselves exercising the privilege of wider realms and fuller use of self? No.

The glories, Rebecca believed; it was for her a time of genuine, deep family satisfactions. The ordainedness, she also believed. It was a time of strict, literal interpretation of the Bible. That she wrote, worked at a "man's" occupation, did not occur to her as contradiction. She carried it on privately, at home, in a woman's way: that is, not as a man would, but fitted in, secondary to family; at the cost of none of her responsibilities to them. And she obeyed the Biblical injunctions: she kept to her place. It was Clarke's right, as husband, to make the decisions, including where they should live. It was natural. She accepted unquestioningly that, whatever their respective capacities, it was Clarke as a man who should be enabled to do his best work, while her ordained situation as woman was to help him toward that end: to be responsible for house, children, the proper atmosphere for his concentration and relaxation—and manage her writing when and as best as she could. Men could have love, home, children, and work, without cost to the work. Not women.

She did not say "Wrong, all wrong." Violations of human potentiality which she refused to accept as natural, as ordained, in *Life in the Iron Mills*, she accepted as natural, as ordained, in the situation of women (including her own).

For all the insights throughout her writings on the narrowness, triviality, drudgery, hurts, restrictions in women's lives, she could not envision women "as they might be." Of their domestic fourteen-hour-a-day, seven-day work week, she did not ask Hetty's question, so terribly punished in "The Wife's Story": "Was [it] for this reality that God made me?" Nor did she apply to her own sex Hugh Wolfe's measure of "a true life," one of "full development of faculties."

WHEN THE high-tide time of family happiness out of which *Pro Aris et Focis* was written receded for Rebecca, she did not see its relationship to the situation of her sex. She knew only that something had gone terribly wrong with her life, her writing.

SHE WAS forty-one now. For eight years—often with exhilaration—she had been juggling cumulative responsibilities, selves, other beings. At last, the children old enough, she was beginning to have some space for time-self. Old aspirations began to rise. Then, once more, she discovered she was pregnant.

The third child ("but the child was a girl"), Nora, was born in 1872.

The following year, Rebecca wrote another revealing "Wife's Story," but this time there is neither terror nor temptation in it: the gift is used—without punishment—for family needs; the anguish is explicit only on the last page.

She called it *Earthen Pitchers*, a seven-part serial in *Scribner's Monthly* (1873 and 1874) about the fate of two young women earning their living professionally at a time when professional women were an extreme rarity.

Jenny, "built for use but not for show," is a no-nonsense journalist, with no pretensions to art.

Men who wanted to stand well with Jenny were wont to talk of the strength of her articles, quite as masculine as if they had been done by a man.

Audrey is a musician—violinist, singer, composer. She has been rigorously training herself since early childhood, eight to ten hours a day, for a life in music. Music "is all there is of me," she says. One of the men in love with her answers:

> "The best of you, I grant, but not all. . . . Half of your nature will be fallow. Besides, what do you know to teach by your art? What experience have you of life?"

On a night of auroral light and wild ocean storm, Audrey's whole-selved concentration on music is momentarily breached by a rousing of desire for a man, for human love. Later, unable to sleep, she goes out again into the storm:

> Now, it seemed to her, she had grown to the age of sea and woods: they had received her into their company; she was one with them. . . . she would have penetrated into the heart of this eternal world if she could; its mysteries, its vastness, its infinite, inaccessible repose. . . . The longing, the hope, which belong to those who are akin with Nature, for which no man has ever found words, oppressed and choked her. "And I," she said, looking up and around her, as one who seeks a familiar face, "I too!"

She knows she must find a way to express this longing, this hope. "Strains of simple powerful harmony, unknown before," come to her. She stays all night by the sea, in what is a transcendent experience. Toward dawn, when "all things seemed waiting, glad, questioning, having accepted her as their own," kingbirds, sandpipers, "fixing their eyes on her in recognition," she floats far out to deep water. It has "the solemnity of a baptism." She knows she has been "summoned by a heavenly call to do her work; forbidden to do any other."

But Kit, the man she loves, is blinded in a train accident. She marries after all.

> During those years, while he was both blind and helpless, . . . [she] supported the family by giving music lessons to all the children in the neighborhood. Her old uncle opposed her bitterly. . . .
>
> "Don't make a market of your birthright," he said, "hide it, bury it in a napkin if you will. You sold yourself, but don't sell that for your own selfish ends, or God will punish you."
>
> "My birthright is to love," said Audrey, and laid her hand on her husband's arm.

Both women are disillusioned in marriage but manage what happiness they can. Jenny's husband is a philanderer, dilettante, poseur, who takes all comforts and luxuries as his due ("Jenny . . . knew all his maxims as she did her alphabet"). As for Audrey,

> No wife could be more loving and cheerful with Kit. Yet, unconsciously, she gives you the impression that she has her own home and her own people elsewhere and will be gone to them presently.

The novel ends by the sea:

> The sun is heat to her now, and the sea, water.

Presently, when evening begins to gather, and the sunset colors the sky and the pools in the marshes behind them, blood-red, and the sea washes into their feet, dark and heavy, with subdued cries and moans, as though all the love and unappeased longing of the world had gone down into it, and sought to find speech in it, Audrey takes up the child, and begins to hush it on her breast, singing a little cradle song, a simple chant with which she was always crooning it to sleep. It is so hopeful, so joyful, so full of the unutterable brooding tenderness of mother's love, that Kit, who cares little for music, finds his heart swell and his eyes dim.

"Your uncle and that Goddard," he observes, "used to think you had a pretty talent for music Audrey. You were going to teach the whole world by your songs, I remember. But that little tune is all you ever made, eh? . . . And nobody ever heard it but Baby and me. However, it's very pretty, very pretty. And it was lucky your uncle taught you as thoroughly as he did. Your scales and notes helped us over a rough place. They served their purpose very well, though your voice is quite gone with teaching."

He strolls on up the beach.

When he was out of sight, a flock of kingbirds fly up from the hedges of bay bushes, and light near her, turning on her their bright black eyes with a curious look of inquiry. When was it they had looked at her so before?

For one brief moment the tossing waves, the sand dunes, the marshes put on their dear old familiar faces. Old meanings, old voices came close to her as ghosts in the sunlight. The blood rushed to her face, her blue eyes lighted. She buried her hands in the warm white sand. She held the long salt grass to her cheeks. She seemed to have come home to them again. "Child," they said to her, as the statues to Mignon, "where hast thou stayed so long?"

It seemed to her that she must answer them. She began to sing, she knew not what. But the tones were discordant, the voice was cracked. Then she knew that whatever power she might have had was quite wasted and gone. She would never hear again the voice that once had called to her.

She rose then, and, taking up her child, went to the house, still looking in its face. Kit joined her, and was dully conscious that she had been troubled. "You're not vexed at what I said down there, eh?" he asked. "You're not really sorry, that you leave nothing to the world but that little song?"

"I leave my child," said Audrey; repeating after awhile, "I leave my child."

Her husband, at least, was sure that she made no moan over that which might have been and was not.

No happy ending. The wife had forsaken her heavenly call, taken up what was "no better work in life for a woman." She had literally made herself a visible Providence for her husband and child. The punishment came anyway. It was her birthright world of art out of which she was cast, whose faces were averted. The death was to the self that had had the power to achieve, the murder had been to her calling, the practice of art which was her life.

HOW MUCH of the disillusion with marriage, the pain pulsing through the strong last chapter and distilled in its ambiguous last sentence, was also Rebecca's, writing in the tenth year of her marriage?

In the ten years she had lost her place in the literary world. She no longer published in the *Atlantic*. The letters from Annie were lapsing. She no longer believed in, acted upon, the possibility of high achievement for herself. It was the price for children, home, love.

Was part of the price, too, that there was no one to whom she could speak the dimensions, the pain, of her loss—not even Clarke (*perhaps not even herself*)?

Hints in *Earthen Pitchers* support the outward facts that this was so. From the beginning, Clarke had not respected her aspiration to art. His own approach was writing as journalistic commodity, not writing as literature. Nor after marriage had he concerned himself with circumstances for her best writing. For all his love, his initial recognition of her potential greatness as writer (her first attraction for him), he had settled easily into what Rebecca too accepted unquestioningly: the "natural," man-wife pattern of *his* ambitions, activities, comforts, needs coming first.

Well, most adults, she observed in an editorial about this time, find themselves having to put their own needs, dreams, aspirations, aside when they take on responsibilities for growing lives. She did not specify male or female. Her husband, at least, whether dully conscious or not, would be sure that she made no moan over that which might have been, and was not.

THE POWER for art might be wasted and gone, but the

power for work remained. The alive social intelligence kept listening to its society, though it might never hear again the voice that once had called. In 1874 she published *John Andross*, calling attention to the control of government by special interests, through bribery of legislators, gangsterism if necessary; and the corruption of character through subservience to wealth. It was the first novel of this kind.

The first year in the new house, she had written another first book of its kind—a defense of the rights of supposedly insane persons. Clarke had told her in his lawyer days of the malign practice whereby family members or enemies could, without notice, commit a sane person as insane to an institution, to be held there incommunicado ("buried alive") for life—simply on the basis of a statement by one cooperative doctor. Now her *Put Out of the Way* (published in *Peterson's* in 1871), along with editorials and articles by Clarke, resulted in getting the Pennsylvania lunacy laws changed.

The Philadelphia Centennial Exposition of 1876 came and went. "Though Clarke was one of the most active managers . . . I was only down there one evening," Rebecca wrote Annie. She was not present, then, when Susan B. Anthony, Elizabeth Cady Stanton, and other women "sat in" at the assembly celebrating that hundredth year of the Declaration of Independence and took over the platform to read their Women's Declaration of Rights.

Rebecca went almost nowhere now. Clarke went everywhere. He was a leading citizen, an increasingly influential man-about-town; his fishing companions included Grover Cleveland. Their social circle consisted of Clarke's friends, many of them theatrical people. The Drews, the Barrymores; when they were in town, Ellen Terry, Sir Henry Irving, Joseph Jefferson, Edwin Booth. Pre-matinee breakfasts at the Davis's became a custom. There is no record that Rebecca went on to the theater with Clarke afterward.

In 1878, *The Nation* reviewed *A Law Unto Herself*:

> Mrs. Rebecca Harding Davis writes stories which can hardly be called pleasant, and which frequently, as in "A Law unto Herself," deal with most unpleasant persons, but there is an undercurrent of recognized aptitude and a capacity for calling a spade a spade which sets her writing in a category far removed from French morality. . . . though she shows bad taste in various ways, or perhaps because of this, she succeeds in giving a truer impression of American conditions than any writer we know except Mr. Howells, while there is a vast difference between his delicately illuminated preparations of our social absurdities and Mrs. Davis's grim and powerful etchings. Somehow she contrives to get the American atmosphere, its vague excitement, its strife of effort, its varying possibilities. Add to this a certain intensity, a veiled indignation at prosperity, and doubt of the honesty of success, and we get qualities which make Mrs. Davis's books individual and interesting if not agreeable.

She did not feel very agreeable. The rasp of asperity characterized her more and more. She wrote the young Kate Field in England:

Don't come home if you are happy there. You can have no idea of the stagnation of . . . all life here. The country is like a man whom somebody is holding by the throat.

In 1881, into this supposed stagnation, Helen Hunt Jackson published her documented denunciation of the genocidal treatment of the American Indian, *A Century of Dishonor* (a first of *its* kind). To the keen disappointment of its author, who regarded her as a still-active champion of the wronged ("I counted on you to bring out the facts as I wanted them brought out"), Rebecca did not review it.

There is a picture of Rebecca taken during this time. The hair is still severely parted in the middle, but now the luxuriant curls are stiff; the eyes, slits; the face clamped; the hands clamped together. She looks old, shrewd, grim, somehow formidable; not at all the ardent young woman who twenty years before had been a Hope in native letters and had had her picture taken before going up North to be welcomed as such.

Oliver Wendell Holmes had not forgotten that younger Rebecca. Richard, now eighteen, stopped by to visit him: "He talked a great deal about Mamma."

Mamma thought a great deal about Richard. "I leave my child," Audrey had said stubbornly at the end of *Earthen Pitchers*, "I leave my child." It was beginning to seem that Rebecca's child might become the fine writer she had not.[39] She encouraged him, with advice still helpful for young writers:

I don't say like Papa, stop writing. God forbid. I would almost as soon say stop breathing, for it is pretty much the same thing. But only to remember that you have not yet conquered your art. You are a journeyman, not a master workman, so if you don't succeed [now] it does not count. The future is what to look to. . . . I've had 30 years experience and I know how much [getting published] depends on the articles suiting the present needs of the magazine, and also on the mood of the editor when he reads it. Develop . . . your dramatic eye, your quick perception of character and of the way character shows itself in looks, tones, dress . . . your keen sympathy with all kinds of people. Add to that your humour. Just in proportion to your feeling more deeply and noticing more keenly, [you will] acquire the faculty of expressing more delicately and powerfully. Not inspiration, practice. A lasting real success takes time and patient steady work.

I had to stop my work to say all this, so goodbye dear old chum.

And mamma went back to her work in which, through habits of years, she seldom stopped to use her advice. Richard went on to become famous.

Her first critical and popular success in years came in 1892 with *Silhouettes of American Life,* her first collection of stories. A strain from *Earthen Pitchers* and from "The Wife's Story" sounds within it: the power for art wasted and gone—but this time there is doubt, was the power ever there?

It was with her precisely as when her heart swelled with a song that ought to silence heaven itself—and she uttered a cracked piping falsetto; or as when years ago, she felt herself inspired with poetry, and had written miserable rhymes—vapid and pretentious.

And there is a significant story, "Anne," of an older woman, a woman in her sixties, who runs away from home. Though she is shrewdly successful in business, and her children patronizingly love her, somewhere else is her heart's country of books and music "and the companionship of thinkers." On the train she sits close enough to overhear a famous poet, a great painter of human suffering, a noted woman reformer, all traveling together. But they prove false, "mere hucksters," who

> had made a trade of art and humanity . . . until they had lost the perceptions of their highest meanings.

The train is wrecked. She is brought back home, "petted like a baby":

> Yet sometimes in the midst of all this comfort and sunshine a chance note of music or the sound of the restless wind will bring an expression into her eyes which her children do not understand, as if some creature unknown to them looked out. . . .
> At such times [she] will say to herself, "Poor Anne!" as of somebody whom she once knew that is dead.
> *Is* she dead?

Probably to the end of her days, a creature unknown to those around her lived on in Rebecca, a secret creature still hungry to know; living (like Audrey) ecstatically in nature, in the sea, summers; (like Anne) "with her own people, elsewhere" in the year-round red-brick house.

Seldom does she appear in the books and stories and articles that kept on and on (so many that it would take several years just to read all she wrote in her lifetime). In her seventies, she still kept grinding them out. This is but a sampling: "Temple of Fame," "Curse of Education," "Ignoble Martyr," "Country Girls in Town," "The Disease of Money-Getting," "Is It All for Nothing?" "In the Gray Cabins of New England" (about the "starved, coffined" lives of spinsters), "New Traits of the New American," "Under the Old Code," "The Black North" (about the furor aroused by President Roosevelt's inviting Booker T. Washington to dine at the White House—nothing so delighted Rebecca as exposing racist hypocrisy), "Recovery of Family Life," "Story of a Few Plain Women," "Undistinguished Americans," "Unwritten History."

SHE DIED in 1910, age seventy-nine, writing almost to the last moment. No literary journal noted her passing. *Life in the Iron Mills* and *Margret Howth* were already so obliterated by 1891, that Eleanor Marx and Edward Aveling, in their *The Working Class Movement in America*, could write:

> . . . one of these days the Uncle Tom's Cabin of Capitalism will be written.
> And here we are tempted to ask, "Where are the American writers of fiction?" With a subject, and such a subject, lying ready to their very hands, clamoring at their very doors, not one of them touches it. . . .

there are no studies of factoryhands and of dwellers in tenement houses; no pictures of those sunk in the innermost depths of the modern *Inferno*.

On the occasion of her death, the *New York Times* *did* resurrect the fact that a half century before—before the Inferno had emerged as the overwhelming dominant of American life—a work on the subject had appeared. In its newsstory-obituary ("Mother of Richard Harding Davis Dies at Son's Home in Mt. Kisco, aged 79"), it told how:

> In 1861 she sent to The Atlantic Monthly a story entitled "Life in the Iron Mills," depicting the grinding life of the working people around her. . . . It attracted attention from all over the country. . . . many thought the author must be a man. The stern but artistic realism of the picture she put alive upon paper, suggested a man, and a man of power not unlike Zola's.

They did not mention that she had preceded Zola by two decades.[40]

The *Dictionary of American Biography* memorializes her in an estimate denying stern and artistic merit altogether:

> . . . without guidance or knowledge of literary art save as she had gained it from voluminous reading, she began early to write fiction. . . . Though often crude and amateurish in workmanship, these stories were nevertheless remarkable productions, distinct landmarks in the evolution of American fiction. Written when the American novel was in all its areas ultra-romantic and

over-sentimental, they are Russian-like in their grim and sordid realism.

Landmarks, unless they loom large in landscapes often visited, tend to become weed-grown tombstones over forgotten dead, noticed only by accident.

Even the sense of landmark has been obliterated. Rebecca Harding Davis is a name known today only to a handful of American Studies people and literary historians. Few have read any of her work; fewer still teach any of it.[41]

MYRIADS OF human beings—those who did the necessary industrial work in the last century—lived and died and little remains from which to reconstruct their perished (vanished) lives. About them, as about so much else, literature was largely silent, and the charge can be levied: *Nowhere am I in it. Unlimn'd, they disappear.*

No picture, poem, statement, passing them to the future . . .[42]

To those of us, descendants of their class, hungry for any rendering of what they were like, of how they lived, Rebecca Harding Davis's *Life in the Iron Mills* is immeasurably precious. Details, questions, Vision, found nowhere else—dignified into living art.

She never wrote anything of its classic quality after.

Once, at Harvard's Widener Library, in that time of my trying to trace what had happened with Rebecca Harding, out of one of her books—*John Andross?*—fell an undated presentation card:

For Mr. C. E. Norton
from R.H.D.
Judge me—not by what I have done, but
by what I have hoped to do.[43]


Poor Rebecca. The cry of every artist (of every human). But Proust is right. There are no excuses in art. Including having been born female in the wrong time/place.

A scanty best of her work is close to the first rank; justifies resurrection, currency, fame. Even that best is botched.

Here or there in even her most slipshod novels, stage-set plots, moldering stories: a grandeur of conception ("touches, grand sweeps of outline"), a breathing character, a stunning insight, a scene as transcendent as any written in her century, also confirm for us what a great writer was lost in her.

Even in the tons of her ephemera, of the topical nonfiction, there is vitality, instructive range—and a fascinating native quality in its combination of radicalism, reaction, prophecy, piecemeal insights, skepticism, idealism, all done up in a kind of exasperated plain-spokenness.

The strong pulse of her work quoted herein evidences that—botched art or not—a significant portion of her work remains important and vitally alive for our time. She is more than landmark, of contemporary interest only to literary historians—though she is that too. There is an untraced indebtedness to her in the rise of realism. She maintained that fiction which incorporates social and economic problems directly, *and in terms of their effects on human beings.*[44]

She was more than realist. In the most scrupulous sense, she followed Emerson's dicta:

> I ask not for the great, the remote, the romantic. . . . I embrace the common, I explore and sit at the feet of the familiar, the low.

> The foolish man wonders at the unusual; the wise man at the usual.

The complexity of that wonder illumines her best pages.

She was not derivative. Her pioneering firsts in subject matter are unequaled. She extended the realm of fiction.

Without intention, she was a social historian invaluable for an understanding access to her time. On her pages are people and situations that are discovery, not only of the past, but of ourselves.

From her work—like *the figure of the mill woman cut in korl, kept hid behind the curtain it is such a rough ungainly thing*—her epoch looks through *with its thwarted life, its mighty hunger, its unfinished work.*

It is time to rend the curtain.

# NOTES

My primary sources have been the writings of Rebecca Harding Davis, everything of hers accessible to me for reading. In addition, I relied on Gerald Langford's *The Richard Harding Davis Years* (New York: Holt, Rinehart & Winston, 1961) for biographical fact (not interpretation); on Helen Woodward Schaeffer's *Rebecca Harding Davis, Pioneer Realist* (an as-yet-unpublished doctoral dissertation: University of Pennsylvania, 1947); on Charles Belmont Davis's edition of *The Adventures and Letters of Richard Harding Davis* (New York: Scribner's Sons, 1917); and, as is evident, on my other reading done over years, related to the period in which she lived.

I first read *Life in the Iron Mills* in one of three water-stained, coverless volumes of bound *Atlantic Monthly*s bought for ten cents each in an Omaha junkshop. I was fifteen. Contributions to those old *Atlantic*s were published anonymously, and I was ignorant of any process whereby I might find the name of the author of this work which meant increasingly more to me over the years, saying "Literature can be made out of the lives of despised people," and "You, too, must write."

No reader I encountered had ever heard of the story, let alone who might have written it. It was not until *The Letters of Emily Dickinson* (Cambridge: Belknap Press) came out in 1958 that, in the reference room of the San Francisco Public Library where I went lunch hours from work to read them, I learned who the author was. Appended to a note from Emily to her sister-in-law

> Will Susan please lend Emily "Life in the Iron Mills"—and accept blossom

was this citation:

> Rebecca Harding Davis's "Life in the Iron Mills" appeared in the April 1861 issue of the *Atlantic Monthly*.

It did not surprise me that the author was of my sex. At once I eagerly looked for other works by her. But there was no Rebecca Harding Davis in the library's card catalogue. It did not occur to me to try the magazine index, as it dated only from the 1890s and I assumed that she had been dead long since. No other library, even had I had time, was accessible to me.

Only when I received an appointment to the Radcliffe Institute in 1962 did I begin to have time and access to other of her work. There they were, in Harvard's Widener Library, in the Cambridge and Boston public libraries: in old volumes, not taken out for years.

So began my knowledge of her contribution and its woeful deterioration; my attempt to understand what had happened to the Rebecca Harding who had once written with such power, beauty, comprehension—genius.

I never envisioned writing of her until Florence Howe and Paul Lauter, to whom I had introduced *Life in the Iron Mills*, suggested that The Feminist Press issue it and that I write the foreword. This is the result. I am not proud of it, but I am not ashamed of it either. If I have quoted so extensively from her work, it is because it is neither readily available nor known. If my essay came to be more biographical interpretation and history than critical afterword, it is because I am convinced that that is what is most needed. I have brought to her life and work my understanding as writer, as avid reader, as feminist-humanist, as woman.

Throughout, *Life in the Iron Mills* appears in italics, as novels do. This is my idiosyncrasy; I consider it to be of that weight.

1. Rebecca Harding Davis's correspondence, some of the correspondence with her, and other references used are scattered through a number of volumes. As I was reading for myself only, until the preparation of this manuscript, and had had no academic training in notation, I copied out material usually without troubling to record exact pages, publishers, dates of publication, sometimes even titles of the books or magazines. This explains the few instances in which the exact source is not cited; but in every case it can be authenticated. Where no source is indicated, and it is Rebecca Harding Davis who is being quoted, the material comes either from correspondence, articles, or is a phrase from

her fiction, usually from *Life in the Iron Mills*—and the context should make the difference clear.

2. From *The Story of an African Farm* (1883; reprint ed., New York: Fawcett Publications, Inc., 1968), p. 162.

A poem quoted by a contemporary, sculptor Harriet Hosmer, puts it thusly:

> Ground down enough
> to flatten and bake into a wholesome crust
> for household uses and properties

In *Eminent Women of the Age* (Hartford, Conn.: S. M. Betts Company, 1869), p. 569. And Elizabeth Cady Stanton wrote in the same book (p. 341) of the far superior seminary she attended: "If there is any one thing on earth from which I pray God to save my daughters, it is a girls' seminary. The two years which I spent in a girls' seminary were the dreariest years of my whole life."

3. From *Bits of Gossip*, a volume of reminiscences published by Rebecca Harding Davis (Boston and New York: Houghton Mifflin, 1904), p. 168. The LeMoyne family home in Washington, Pennsylvania, has been kept as a historical museum, centering mostly on Dr. Francis LeMoyne.

4. Booth Tarkington on Richard Harding Davis:

> To the college boy of the 90's, he was the beau ideal. His stalwart good looks were as familiar to us as were

those of our own football captain; we knew his face as we knew the face of the President of the United States, but we infinitely preferred Davis's.

Davis was the model for Charles Dana Gibson's man-about-town, appearing over and over in the famous Gibson Girl drawings. Later, during his roving correspondent days, he was often seen in press photographs with presidents, warring generals, revolutionary leaders, explorers.

5. Her father may have preferred to keep her home, as fathers of the time—including some famous fathers—often did. Consider Browning, Bronte, Dickinson, Evans (father of George Eliot).

6. Quotations in this and the next five paragraphs are from *David Gaunt*, *Margret Howth*, *Earthen Pitchers*, *John Andross*, and *A Law Unto Herself*.

7. From a letter by the young Harriet Beecher (Stowe) in somewhat similar circumstances at about the same age. She wrote her friend Georgianna:

> All that is enthusiastic, all that is impassioned in admiration of nature, of writing, of character, or in the emotions of affection, I have felt with vehement and absorbing intensity—felt till my mind is exhausted and seems to be sinking into deadness. Half of my time I am glad to remain in a listless vacancy, to busy myself with tasks, since thought is pain and emotion is pain.

From *Life and Letters of Harriet Beecher Stowe*, edited by Annie Fields (1898; reprint ed., Detroit: Gale Research, 1970).

8. Lucy Stone in a debate at Antioch:

> The present regime to which custom dooms the sex: steel-ribbed corsets with hoops, heavy skirts, trains; high heels; panniers, chignons and dozens of hairpins sticking in their scalps; cooped up in the house year after year with no exhilarating exercise, no hopes, aims nor ambitions.

Quoted in Alice Stone Blackwell's *Lucy Stone, Pioneer of Women's Rights* (Boston: Little, Brown and Co., 1920).

9. Which it was not. Though Hawthorne complained in a letter to his publisher of "the damned mob of female scribblers," the field was dominated by men: all editors, publishers, and staff were men; the overwhelming number of novels, stories, articles, were still being written by men. The comparatively few women writers were conspicuous because they were a new phenomenon, for the first time in any numbers successful, recognized. And the Women's Rights movement had focused attention on women. The 1850s was the decade of Whitman, Thoreau, Melville, Hawthorne, Dana, Emerson, Lowell, Holmes, Whittier, though not all had popular fame.

Fred Pattee, the literary historian who affixed the label "feminine fifties," writes that he did so because ten words characterized the decade: "Fervid, fevered, furious, fatuous, fertile, feeling, florid, furbelowed, fighting, funny"—and the "single adjective that would combine tham all" is "feminine." From *The Feminine Fifties* (New York: Appleton-Century, 1940).

10. Van Wyck Brooks said of it in *New England: Indian Summer* (New York: E. P. Dutton & Co., 1940), p. 12: "The supremacy of *The Atlantic* was unquestioned. To have published . . . in it . . . was to be known among writers all over the country. It was a force . . . setting the critical standard and spreading suggestions."

To Emily Dickinson it was "a temple." To appear in it was a true accolade, and guaranteed a wide and distinguished audience. It was the first to use the expression "realism." One of its editors, Thomas Wentworth Higginson, a great and influential male champion of women's rights, actively promoted the development and publication of women writers. An *Atlantic* article of his—"Women and the Alphabet"—was credited with resulting directly in the founding of Smith College and the opening of the University of Michigan to women.

11. Insofar as I know, furnace fires had burned but three times before in American literature: in that small hillside lime kiln where Hawthorne's Ethan Brand incinerated himself for his Unpardonable Sin—the separation of the intellect from the heart; in the "try works" on the "red hell" of the "Pequod" in Melville's *Moby Dick*; and in occasional lines in Whitman's "Crossing Brooklyn Ferry," "A Song for Occupations," and "Song of Joys":

O to work . . . forging iron,
Foundry casting, the foundry itself, the rude high
    roof, the ample and shadow'd space,
The furnace, the hot liquid pour'd out and running.

Whitman's descriptions are noticeably different from those of *Life in the Iron Mills*.

12. Contrast the few critiques of the machine, of industry, of materialism, with that in *Life in the Iron Mills* (and *Margret Howth*). Instead of "things are in the saddle and ride mankind," Rebecca Harding Davis alone showed how the makers of things were being ridden.

13. A picture of cotton mills as a kind of industrial paradise was the vision impressed on the public, primarily by the widely distributed and famous *Lowell Offering* of the 1840s, in which poems and stories by Lowell, Waltham, and Chicopee mill "girls" appeared. These young women *were* "hungry to know," did meet in Lowell Improvement Circles to study after their thirteen-hour workday, but the conditions under which they worked and their reactions to it were not allowed to appear in the heavily edited magazine. Their own later publications, *The Factory Girl*, *Valentine Offering*, and *The Voice of Industry* (organ of the Female Labor Reform Association) received no attention in literary circles.

14. Published in the *Atlantic* in January 1862. In this remarkable story, a century ahead of its time in its

understanding of racism and the rights of the enslaved to freedom, the white Southern guilt-fear, the fear that the oppressed when free will behave as oppressively, breaks out at the end. What had been understood as "the same heroic dream that bade Tell and Garibaldi lift their hands to God" for freedom becomes an animal lust for revenge, for being master, and for the young sister of Lamar. In contradiction, in *Bits of Gossip* (p. 185) Rebecca points out that "during the Civil War the women and children of the South were wholly under the protection of their slaves, and I never have heard of a single instance in which they abused a trust."

15. Famed as a wilderness explorer, the man who had won the popular, if not the electoral, vote for the presidency in 1856, Frémont was being maneuvered out of the command. "The incarnation of the chivalric and noble side of Abolitionism"; "simple, high-bred, courteous; always at a white heat of purpose" (Rebecca's words), he was suspect. The fall before, when in command of the Missouri Territory, he had ordered the slaves therein freed, the first and only such order of emancipation. The action was annulled by Lincoln.

16. Quotations from Margaret Fuller appear throughout Rebecca's writings.

17. The power of reticence again. The bitterness with which Rebecca felt this restriction is revealed by her obsessed fascination with Ellen, "a girl of the laboring

classes," who wandered penniless and freely through state after state, looking for a soldier brother who had disappeared. In later years, Rebecca wrote Ellen's story not once, but twice, the second time as fiction. The first was "Ellen" (*Peterson's*, 1863); the second in *Atlantic* (July 1865).

18. The quotations in the account of Rebecca's New England visit, if not otherwise footnoted, come from *Bits of Gossip*.

19. "Saw Miss Rebecca Harding, author of *Margret Howth*, which has made a stir, and is very good. A handsome, fresh, quiet woman, who says she never had any troubles, though she writes about woes. I told her I had had lots of troubles, so I write jolly tales; and we wondered why we each did so." From her diary, May 1862, in *Louisa May Alcott, Her Life, Letters and Journals*, edited by Ednah Chaney (Boston: Little, Brown, 1928), p. 106.

20. Annie Fields's "angel in the house" contribution to American literature (and British-American literary relations) has never been assessed. For half a century, "writers as famous as Thackeray and Dickens, down to starving poets from the western prairies" came and stayed there; friendships were formed, cemented. She was Sarah Orne Jewett's closest friend. They invariably summered together, and it was she who introduced Willa Cather to Jewett. There is a memorable tribute to

Annie Fields in Cather's *Not Under Forty*, and a book on her by Mark de Wolfe Howe, *Memories of a Hostess*. After Fields's death, Annie published two books of poems, *Under the Olive* and *The Singing Shepherd and Other Poems*, as well as *The Life and Letters of Harriet Beecher Stowe* and a book of reminiscences, *Authors and Friends*.

21. "Mr. Emerson stood listening, his head sunk on his breast, with profound submissive attention, but Hawthorne sat astride of a chair, his arms folded on the back, his chin dropped on them, and his laughing, sagacious eyes watching us, full of mockery."

22. *The Flowering of New England* (New York: E. P. Dutton and Co., 1936), p. 546.

23. Hawthorne died in May 1864, within two years of their meeting.

24. "O Annie," she wrote on returning, "the inexpressible loathing I have for it [the war]. If you could only see the other side enough to see the wrong, the tyranny on both. I could tell you things I know that would make your heart sick."

25. *Atlantic* had paid $200 for the six-part *Margret Howth*, $400 for the book publication of it.

26. Published in *Atlantic* (May, June, and July 1863).

The comment is made in the story that contrary to expressed attitudes that women are angels, while being treated as idiots, "in these rough & tumble days, we'd better give 'em their places as flesh and blood, with exactly the same wants and passions as men."

27. Rebecca's description of Lucretia Mott appears in *Bits of Gossip*. The full description is recommended as being of special interest for biographers, students, and historians:

> Lucretia Mott [is] one of the most remarkable women that this country has ever produced. . . . No man . . . had a more vigorous brain or ready eloquence. . . . Even in extreme old age she was one of the most beautiful women I have ever seen . . . a little, vivid, delicate creature, alive with magnetic power. . . . that charming face with its wonderful luminous eyes . . . is as real to me at this moment as ever. . . .When you were with [her], you were apt to think of her as the mother and housekeeper, rather than as the leader of a party. . . . Her fingers never were quiet. Until the day of her death she kept up the homely, domestic habits of her youth.

28. Margaret Fuller in *Women in the Nineteenth Century*. This original observation continues on to say: ". . . from which [s]he can only be cured by a time of isolation which gives the renovating fountains time to rise up."

29. In March, Clarke was ill, and Rebecca wrote Annie of herself: "And then I was just enough ailing in mind

to be nervous and irritable, a stupid desire to be quiet and forgotten. Do you never feel as if every faculty has been rasped and handled unbearably and must rest?"

30. Among others: Dorothy Canfield Fisher's "Babushka Farnham," in *Fables for Parents* (New York: Harcourt Brace, 1937); Mary Grey Hughes's "The Thousand Springs," in her collection so entitled (Orono, Maine: Puckerbrush Press, 1970); Elizabeth Stuart Phelps's *The Story of Avis* (Boston: J. R. Osgood & Co., 1877).

31. The wound, the self-belittlement to a woman, involved in feeling that a male child is more worthy, preferable to a female child, is written of for the first time here.

32. Rosa Bonheur (1822–1899) was the most famous woman painter of her time. She painted animals exclusively.

33. *Galaxy* was changing its format, wanted the install-ments cut. "It was only at your request that I gave it to Galaxy to publish serially," Rebecca protested in a different tone from the shaken Rebecca to Fields six years before.

> You must allow me the feeling which the humblest workman has for his work. . . . Whether it mutilates the story or not [seems] a secondary consideration to you.

But primary to her. To no avail. Her situation as con-tracted-for-employee was made clear. They cut, and sometimes she cut.

34. It is Anny, Nat's wife, speaking to Rosslyn, a white woman:

> "De debt de whites owes us is to give us a chance to show what stuff's in us. . . . De next five years is de trial day for us. . . . Your chile has every chance open to him; but dar's few schools in de country beside dem kept by de Quakers dat will admit a cullored boy or girl. Dey calls us lazy an' idle, but wher's de mechanics' shop or factory open for Tom to learn a trade? What perfession is free to him? His hands is tied. His father giv' his blood free for de country," proudly. "He has a right to ask de chance for his son dat neber was gib to himself!"
>
> "The negroes will be given a vote," confidently. [This is Rosslyn.]
>
> "I don' see what real use to dem dat is yet," gravely, "only to make dem feel dey is men. It's edication my people needs, and ways for work. It's de fever time wid 'em now in de Souf; dey's mad for de chance to learn. Ole men an' young stretch out dere hands for de books. It won't last if dey're balked now. . . ."

35. He puts the horrors of insurrection into perspective:

> De white people in de Souf, dey want der own guver'ment, an' dey fights for it wid artillery an' Par-rott guns, an' kills tousands, an' dey calls it war; an' Nat Turner, he want his freedom, an' he fights wid knives an' pikes, an' sech wepons as he gets, an' kills fifty odd, an dey calls it murder.

36. Margaret says to a house slave who asks her what freedom does for blacks up North:

> "It does nothing for them" carelessly, remembering to whom she was speaking. . . . "They are like Mose. He does light work here; he shaves beards, or whitewashes walls, or steals; he does the same in Philadelphia. He is thick-lipped and thriftless and affectionate, go where he will; only in the South they hunt him with dogs, and in the North they calculate how many years of competition with the white race it will need to sweep him and his like off of the face of the earth."

37. Harriet Beecher Stowe wrote to her later:

> The *Nation* has no sympathy with any deep & high moral movement—no pity for human infirmity. It is a sneering respectable middle-aged sceptic who says I take my two glasses & my cigar daily . . . but dont mind them & dont hope for a sympathetic word from them *ever*.

38. Yes, Rebecca, who did not do much resting in her husband's house, said "rest." In "The Wife's Story," she also uses the word "rest": "To nestle down into this man's heart and life! To make his last years that warm Indian summer day! I could do it! I! What utter rest there were in that."

39. See footnote 4 on Richard Harding Davis. Though his multitude of books have none of the intrinsic merit and interest of his mother's, he was one of the famous writers of his time, a man of action and letters whose

example supposedly influenced Hemingway and John Reed.

He wrote Rebecca almost every day of her life, and took care of her the last few years. Before she died, she wrote him: "Some day you'll know what it [is] to be old & how your heart just aches with happiness when people you love—love you." And in another letter: "O Dick . . . I want you always to know how happy you make me in my old age."

As for Nora, his sister ("but the child was a girl"), neither Rebecca nor Clarke seem to have encouraged her to much of anything. Nora (Noll) was subject to "nervous illnesses"; this letter from Rebecca to Richard is revealing:

> The woman who was managing [a recreation evening on board ship] came to Nora & said "Wont you play for us?" "Thank you I don't play" Noll said. "Then you sing?" "No I dont sing." "Perhaps you recite?" "I cant recite." "Oh then you will tell a story." "No I cant tell stories." "And yet," said the woman turning to the listening room, "and yet she is Richard Harding Davis's sister!" Then everyone talked & said how they had read every word you wrote.

40. The newsstory-obituary erred as to when *Life in the Iron Mills* was written, saying that Rebecca "was less than 20 years old." The lead paragraph and the account as a whole gave as much space to her family as to her:

> Mrs. Rebecca Harding Davis, 79 years old, widow of the late L. Clarke Davis, at one time editor of The Philadelphia Public Ledger, mother of Richard

Harding Davis, the novelist and dramatist, and herself a novelist and editorial writer of power, died here to-night of heart disease.

41. In the last year, xeroxed copies of *Life in the Iron Mills* have begun to circulate and have been used in classes here and there. I originally taught it at Amherst College in 1969.

42. From Walt Whitman's "Yonnondio."

43. C. E. Norton was Charles Eliot Norton, editor, man of literature, Harvard professor. He left his library to that university.

44. Only Elizabeth Stuart Phelps, herself largely forgotten, acknowledges the debt, the influence. In her reminiscences she pays tribute to Rebecca as "writing with an ardor that was human, and a passion that was art." Phelps's "The Twelfth of January" (*Atlantic*, November 1868), in which 112 mill girls are burned to death in a textile mill fire (an actual incident), and her *Silent Partner* (1871) were directly inspired by Rebecca's work. So, less directly, was *The Story of Avis*.

# THE WIFE'S STORY

I will tell you the story of my life, since you ask it; for, though the meaning of the life of any woman of my character would be the same, I believe, the facts of mine, being sharp and compressed, may make it, perhaps, more apparent. It will be enough for me to give you the history of one day,—that of our first coming to Newport; for it seems to me as if it held and spoke out plainly whatever gist and significance there was in all the years for me. I know many people hold the theory, that once in every life God puts the stuff of which He has made the man or woman to the test, gives the soul a chance of a conscious fight with that other Power to win or lose itself, once for all. I do not know: it seems but just that one should be so left, untrammelled, to choose between heaven and hell: but who can shake off trammels,—make themselves naked of their birth and education? I know that on that day when the face of my fate changed, I myself was conscious of no inward master-struggle: the great Life above and Life below pressed no closer on me, seemed to wait on no word of mine. It was a busy, vulgar day enough: each passing moment occupied me thoroughly. I did not look through them for either God or Death; and as for the deed I did, I had been drifting to that all my life: it began when I was a pampered, thin-blooded baby, learning the alphabet from blocks on my mother's lap; then years followed, succulent to satiety for my hungry brain and stimulated tastes; a taint of hereditary selfishness played its part, and so the end came. Yet I know that on that day I entered the gate through which there is no returning: for, believe me, there are such ways and gates in life; every day, I see more clearly how far and how immovably the paths into those other worlds abut into this, and I know that I, for one, have gone in, and the door is closed behind me. There is no going back for me into that long-ago time. Only He who led me here knows how humbly and through what pain I dared to believe this, and dare to believe that He did lead me,—that it was by no giddy, blear-sighted free-will of my own that I arrived where I stand today.

It was about eighteen months after my marriage that we came to Newport. But let me go back a few weeks to one evening when my husband first told me of the failure of the house in which his property was invested; for it was then, I think, that the terror and the temptation which had beset my married life first took a definite shape and hold on me.

It was a cool September evening, I remember: a saffronish umber stain behind the low Hudson hills all that was left of the day's fresh and harvest-scented heat; the trails of black smoke from the boats against the sky, the close-shut cottages on the other shore, the very red cows coming slowly up from the meadow-pool, looking lonesome and cold in the sharp, blue air. In the library, however, there was a glow of warmth and light, as usual where Doctor Manning sat. He had been opening the evening's mail, and laid the last letter on the table, taking off his glasses in his slow, deliberate way.

"It is as we feared," turning to me. "It's quite gone, Hester, quite. I'll have to begin at the beginning again. It would have been better I had not trusted the whole to Knopps,—yes."

I said nothing: the news was not altogether unexpected. He took off his wig, and rubbed his head slowly, his eyes fixed on my face with some anxious, steady inquiry, which his tones did not express.

"I'll go back to Newport. Rob's there. I'll get a school again. You did not know I taught there when I was a young man?"

"No."

I knew nothing of my husband's youth. Miss Monchbard, his ward, who was in the room, did, however; and after waiting for me a moment to go on, she said, cheerfully,—

"The boys will be men now, Sir. Friends ready waiting. And different sort of friends from any we have here, eh?"

He laughed.

"Yes, Jacky, you're right. Yes. They've all turned out well, even those Arndts. Jim Arndt used to trot you on his knee on the school-house steps, when you were a baby. But he was a wild chap. He's in the sugar-trade, Rob writes me. But they'll always be boys to me, Jacky,—boys."

His head dropped, with a smile still on his mouth, and he began fingering his scanty beard, as was his habit in his fits of silent musing. Jacqueline looked at him satisfied, then turned to me. I do not know what she saw upon my face, but she turned hastily away.

"It's a town with a real character of its own, Newport, Mrs. Manning,"—trying to make her coarse bass voice gentle. "You'll understand it better than I. New-York houses, now, even these on the Hudson, hint at nothing but a satisfied animal necessity. But there, with the queer dead streets, like a bit of the old-time world, and the big salt sea"—She began to stammer, as usual, and grow confused. "It's like looking out of some far-gone, drowsy old day of the Colonies, and yet feeling life and eternity fresh and near to you."

I only smiled civilly, by way of answer. Jacqueline always tried me. She was Western-born, I a New-Englander; and every trait about her, from the freedom with which she hurled out her opinions to the very setting-down of her broad foot, jarred on me as a something boorish and reckless. Her face grew red now.

"I don't say what I want exactly," she hesitated. "I only hoped you'd like the town, that it would reconcile—There's crabs there," desperately turning to Teddy, who was playing a furtive game of marbles under the table, and grabbing him by the foot. "Come here till I tell you about the crabs."

I remember that I got up and went out of the low window on to the porch, looking down at the quiet dun shadows and the slope of yellowed grass leading to the river, while Jacky and the boy kept up a hurly-burly conversation about soldier-crabs that tore each other's legs off, and purple and pink sea-roses that ate raw meat, and sea-spiders like specks of blood in the rocks. My husband laughed once or twice, helping Jacky out with her natural history. I think it was the sound of that cheery, mellow laugh of his that fermented every bitter drop in my heart, and brought clearly before me for the first time the idea of the course which I afterwards followed. I thrust it back then, as if it had been a sneer of the Devil's at all I held good and pure. What was there in the world good and pure for me but the man sitting yonder, and the thought that I was his wife? And yet—I had an unquiet brain, of moderate power, perhaps, but which had been forced and harried and dragged into exertion every moment of my life, according to the custom with women in the States from which I came. Every meanest hint of a talent in me had been nursed, every taste purged, by the rules of my father's clique of friends. The chance of this was all over,—had been escaping since my marriage-day. Now I clearly saw the life opening before me. What would taste or talent be worth in the coarse struggle we were about to begin for bread and butter? "Surely, we have lost something beyond money," I thought, looking behind into the room, where my husband was quietly going back to the Arndts in quest of food for reflection, and Jacky prosed on about sea-anemones. I caught a glimpse of my sallow face in the mirror: it was full of a fierce disgust. Was their indifference to this loss a mere torpid ignorance of the actual brain- and soul-wants it would bring on us, or did they really look at life and accept its hard circumstances from some strange standing-ground of which I knew nothing? I had not become acclimated to the atmosphere of my husband's family in the year and a half that I had been his wife. He had been married before; there were five children, beginning at Robert, the young preacher at Newport, and ending with Teddy, beating the drum with his fists yonder on the table; all of them, like their father, Western-born; with big, square-built frames, and grave, downright-looking faces; simple-hearted, and much given, the whole party, to bursts of hearty laughter, and a habit of perpetually joking with each other. There might be more in them than this, but I had not found it: I doubted much if it were worth the finding. I came from a town in Massachusetts, where, as in most New-England villages, there was more mental power than was needed for the work that was to be done, and which reacted constantly on itself in a way which my husband called unwholesome; it was no wonder, therefore, that these people seemed to me but clogs of flesh, the mere hands by which the manual work of the world's progress was to be accomplished. I had hinted this to Doctor Manning one day, but he only replied by the dry, sad smile with which it had become his habit of late to listen to my speculations. It had cost me no pain thus to label and set aside his children: but for himself it was different; he was my husband. He was the only thing in the world which I had never weighed and valued to estimate how much it was worth to me: some feeling I could not define had kept me from it until now. But I did it that evening: I remember how the cool river-air blew in the window-curtain, and I held it back, looking steadily in at the thick-set, middle-aged figure of the man sitting there, in the lamp-light, dressed in rough gray: peering at the leather-colored skin, the nervous features of the square face, at the scanty fringe of iron-gray whisker, and the curly wig which he had bought after we were married, thinking to please me, at the brown eyes, with the gentle reticent look in them belonging to a man or beast who is thorough "game"; taking the whole countenance as the metre of the man; going sharply over the salient points of our life together, measuring myself by him, as if to know—what? to know what it would cost me to lose him. God be merciful to me, what thought was this? Oh, the wrench in heart and brain that came then! A man who has done a murder may feel as I did while I stood for the next half-hour looking at the red lights of the boats going up and down the Hudson, in the darkening fog.

After a while Teddy came waddling out on the porch, in his usual uncouth fashion, and began pulling at my cape.

"You're getting cold, mother. Come in. Come!"

I remember how I choked as I tried to answer him, and, patting his gilt-buttoned coat, took the fat chapped little hands in mine, kissing them at last. I was so hungry for affection that night! I would have clung to a dog that had been kind to me. I thought of the first day Doctor Manning had brought him to me, in this same comical little jacket, by the way, and the strangely tender tone in which he had said,—"This is your mother, boy. He's as rough as a bear, Hetty, but he won't give you trouble or pain. Nothing shall give you pain, if I"—Then he stopped. I never heard that man make a promise. If he had come out instead of Teddy on the porch that night, and had spoken once in the old tone, calling me "Hetty," God knows how different all that came after would have been. The motherless boy, holding himself up by my knees, was more sturdy than I that night, and self-reliant: never could have known, in his most helpless baby-days, the need with which I, an adult woman, craved a cheering word, and a little petting.

Jacqueline came behind me and pinned a woollen shawl around my neck, patting my shoulders in her cozy, comfortable fashion.

"None of your dark river-fogs at Newport," she laughed. "The sea-air has the sweep of half the world to gather the cold and freshness in, and it makes even your bones alive. Your very sleep is twice as much sleep there as anywhere else."

Jacky's rough voice was like the cuckoo's: it always prophesied pleasant weather. She went in again now, and sat down on her little sewing-chair. The low, rolling fogs outside, and the sharp September wind rattling the bare branches of the orchard-trees and the bushes on the lawn, only made the solid home-look of comfort within warmer and brighter. There was a wood-fire kindled on the library-hearth, and its glow picked out red flushes of light on the heavy brown curtains, and the white bust of Psyche, and a chubby plaster angel looking down. Jacky, rocking and sewing, her red mouth pursed up, half whistling, suited the picture, somehow, I could not but feel, mere lump and matter though she might be. There was something fresh and spicy about her. I never had been impressed so justly by her as on that night. Rough, perhaps, but it was a pure roughness: everything about the girl had been clean since she was born, you felt, from the paint of the house where she lived to the prayer her nurse had taught her. Her skin was white and ruddy, her blue eyes clear and full of honesty, her brown curls crisp and unoiled. She could not reason, maybe; but she was straightforward and comfortable: every bone in her roly-poly little figure forgot to be a bone, and went into easy cushions of dimpled flesh. If ever Jacky died and went into a more spiritual world, she would be sure to take with her much of the warmth and spring and vigor of this. She had drawn her chair close to Doctor Manning's, where the flickering light touched the soft woollen folds of her dress and the bit of crimson ribbon at her throat. He liked bright colors, like most men of his age. It was a pretty picture.

I turned and looked down at the river again, shivering,—trying to think of the place and all we were leaving. I did not wonder that it cost the others little to give up the house: it meant but little to them. Doctor Manning had bought it just before we were married, being then a square chocolate-colored farm-house, and we had worked our own whims on it to make it into a home, thrusting out a stout-pillared big porch at one side, and one or two snug little bay-windows from my sewing-room. There was a sunny slope of clover down to the river, a dusky old apple and plum orchard at the left, and Mary's kitchen-garden on the right, with a purblind old peacock strutting through the paths, showing its green and gold. Not much in all this: nothing to please Jacky's artist and poet sense, if she had any. But—I held on to the porch-railings now, drumming with my fingers, as I thought of it. It was all the childhood *I* had ever known. He brought me there the day we were married, and until August—six months—we had been there alone. I could hear his old nag Tinder neighing now, in the stable where we used to go every evening to feed and rub him down: for I went with Daniel, as I called him, then, everywhere, even to consult his mason or farm-hands. He used to stand joking with them a minute after the business was over, in an unwonted fashion for him, and then scramble into the buggy beside me, and drive off, his fresh, bright eye turned to the landscape as if enjoying it for the first time.

"God bless you, Hetty!" he used to say, "this is putting new blood into my veins."

Generally, in those long rides, I used to succeed in coaxing him imperceptibly back to talk of his life in South America,—not only that I liked to hear this new phase of wild adventuring life, but my own blood would glow and freshen to see the fierce dare-devil look come back into the eye, and the shut teeth of the grave, laconic old Doctor. People did not know the man I had married,—no; and I would draw in closer to his shaggy coat, and spur him on to his years of trading in the West, and later in this State. He had a curious epigrammatic way of talking that I have noticed in a less degree in many Western men: coming at the marrow and meaning of a scene or person in his narration with a sheer subtilized common-sense, a tough appreciation of fact beyond theory, and of its deeper, juster significance, and a dramatic aptness for expression. Added to all this, my husband's life had been compacted, crowded with incident; it had saddened and silenced his nature abnormally; this was the first break: a going back to what he might have been, such as his children were now.

"I never talked to any one before, Hetty," he said thoughtfully once, as we were driving along, after a few moments' silence. "I feel as if I had got breath, this late in the day, that I never expected, for whatever thought was in me,—and—whatever love."

He turned away his face, crimson at this. He was as strangely reticent and tender on some points as a woman. So seldom he put his love into words! That time I remember how the tears suddenly blinded me, when I heard him, and my fingers grew unsteady, holding the reins. I was so happy and proud. But I said nothing: he would not have liked it.

Of one time in his life Doctor Manning had never

talked to me: of his earlier youth; when he was married before. He was not a man of whom you could ask questions; yet I had hinted an inquiry once or twice in his presence, but only by a change of color and a strange vague restlessness had he shown that he understood my drift of meaning. Soon after that, his eldest son, Robert, came to see his father's new wife, and stayed with us a day or two. He was a short, thickly built young man, with heavy jaws and black hair and eyes,—keen eyes, I soon felt, that were weighing and analyzing me as justly, but more shrewdly than ever his father had done. The night before he went away he came up to the porch-step where I sat, and said abruptly,—

"I am satisfied, and happy to go now."

"I am glad of that," I said earnestly; for the tenderness of the son to the father had touched me.

"Yes. You cannot know the dread I had of seeing you. I knew the risk he ran in laying his happiness in any woman's hands at his hour of life. But it was hard he never should know a home and love like other men,"—his voice unsteady, and with an appealing look.

"He never shall need it," I said, quietly.

"You think not?"—his eyes on the ground. "At all events,"—after a pause,—"he is resting like a child now: it will not be easy to startle him to any harsh reality, and," looking up, "I hope God may deal with you, Mrs. Manning, as you deal with my father. Forgive me," as I began to speak, "you do not know what this is to me. It makes me rough, I know. I never yet have forgiven the woman that"—His mother? He caught the look, stopped, pushed his hair back, caught his breath. "One thing let me say," after a moment's silence. "You do not know my father. If he wakens to find his wife is not what he thinks her, it will be too late for me to warn you then. He has been hurt sore and deeply in his life. Your chance is but once."

I did not reply to Robert Manning, nor was I offended: there was too much solemnity in his coarseness. The man's affection for his father was as part of his life-blood, I believed.

My husband came to me when he saw Robert go, and loosened my hands from my face. I clung to him as I never did before.

"What is this hurt he talks of in your life, Daniel? Will I be enough to take it out? Will I?"

He laughed, a low, constrained laugh, holding my shoulders as if I were a bit of a child.

"God knows you are enough, Hetty. I never thought He'd send me this. Rob has been talking to you? He"—

"He is bitter."

"He loves me,—poor Rob!"

"Tell me of those people that hurt you, as he says."

It was a prurient, morbid curiosity that had seized me. A sort of shiver ran over his frame.

"Eh, what, Hetty?"—in a low voice. "Let that go, let that go,"—standing silent a moment, looking down. "Why would we bring them back, and hack over the old dead faults? Had she no pain to bear? We couldn't find that out to speak for her. But God knows it."

I might have known how my question would have

ended; for, always, he covered over the ill-doing of others with a nervous haste, with the charity of a man himself sharply sensitive to pain.

"It is healthful to go back to past pain," I said, half dissatisfied.

"Is it so?"—doubtfully, as he turned away with me. "I don't know, child. Now and then He has to punish us, or cut out a cancer maybe. But for going back to gloat over the cure or the whiplash—No; it will keep us busy enough to find good air and food, every minute for itself"; and, with a ruddy, genial smile, he had stopped and kissed my forehead.

A year had passed since that night. I was standing on the same porch, but I was alone now. My husband sat a few feet from me in his old easy-chair, but no gulf could have parted us so wide and deeply. Robert Manning had said I would have but one chance. Well, I had had it, and it was gone. So I stood there, looking quietly at him and Jacky and the boy. The child had pushed his father's wig off, and his bare head with its thin iron-gray hair fell forward on his breast, resting on Teddy's sleeping cheek. I saw now how broad and sad the forehead was,—the quiet dignity on the whole face. Yet it had been such a simple-hearted thing to do,—to buy that wig to please me! One of those little follies the like of which would never come again.

I went in and sat down as usual, apart, throwing aside from my neck the shawl which Jacky had pinned there, loathing anything she had touched, so real and sharp was the thought about her become, as if the evening's fog and cold had lent it a venomous life. They had made a quiet cozy picture before, which had bitterly brought back our first married days, but it was broken up now. The Doctor's three boys came lumbering in, with muddy shoes, game-bags, and the usual fiery faces and loud jokes after their day's sport. Jacky threw down her sewing and went out to see the squirrels drawn, and the Doctor smoothed Teddy's hair, looking after them with a pleased smile. One of the rarest sparkles of our daily life! It was a year since Doctor Manning had brought his children home. They filled the house. Musing on the past now, and trying to look at that year calmly, while I sat by the fire, my husband would fade back in the picture into an unmeaning lay-figure. Was this my fault? Could I help it, if God had made me with a different, clearer insight into life and its uses than these people with their sound beef and muscle, their uncouth rejoicing in being alive? There was work enough in them: a broad-fisted grappling with the day's task or obstacle, a drinking of its pain or success into their slow brains, but nowhere the metre to note the soul's changes, nor the eye to speculate on them. "No," my husband had said to me one day, "we Western people have the mass of this country's appointed work to do, so we are content that God should underlie the hypotheses. We waste no strength in guesses at the reason why."

I remember how intolerably the days of that year dragged even in memory, as I sat there trying to judge them fairly,—how other years of my life thrust them aside, persistently, as foreign, alien to me. These others were to me home,—the thoughts that had held me nearest the divine life: I went back to them, my eyes wet, and my heart sick under my weak lungs. The little village of Concord, away up yonder, where I was born,—I was glad to have been born there: thinking how man not only had learned there to stand self-poised and found himself God, but Nature herself seemed there to stop and reflect on her own beauty, and so root deeper in the inner centre. The slow-dropping river, the thoughtful hills, the very dust-colored fern that covers its fields, which might grow in Hades, so breathless and crisp it is, came back to me with a glamour of quiet that night. The soul had space to grow there! remembering how its doors of thought stood wider open to welcome truth than anywhere else on earth. "The only object in life is to grow." It was my father's,—Margaret Fuller's motto. I had been nursed on it, I might say. There had been a time when I had dreamed of attaining Margaret's stature; and as I thought of that, some old subtile flame stirred in me with a keen delight. New to me, almost; for, since my baby was born, my soul as well as my body had been weak and nauseated. It had been so sharp a disappointment! I had intended my child should be reared in New England: what I had lacked in gifts and opportunities he should possess: there was not a step of his progress which I had not mapped out. But the child was a girl, a weazen-faced little mortal, crying night and day like any other animal. It was an animal, wearing out in me the strength needed by-and-by for its mental training. I sent it to a nurse in the country. Her father had met the woman carrying it out to the wagon, and took it in his arms. "Eh? eh? is it so, little lass?" I heard him say. For days after that he looked paler, and his face had a quiet, settled look, as if he had tested the world and was done with it. The days of Tinder and the paddock and the drives were long gone then. I do not remember that after this he ever called me Hetty. But he was cheerful as ever with the boys, and, the week after, Jacky came.

Why did I think of all this now? Some latent, unconscious jar of thought brought suddenly before me a scene of many years before, a damp spring morning in Paris, when I had gone to Rosa Bonheur's studio, just out of the city, to see her "Horse Fair": the moist smell of jonquils; the drifting light clouds above the Seine, like patches of wool; but most, the peculiar life that seemed to impregnate the place itself, holding her, as it were, to her own precise niche and work in the world,—the sharply managed lights, the skins, trappings, her disguises on the walls, the stables outside, and the finished work before us, instinct with vigor and an observation as patient as keen. I remembered how some one had quoted her as saying, "Any woman can be a wife or mother, but this is my work alone."

I, too, had my gift: but one. But again the quick shiver of ecstasy ran through me;—it was my power, my wand with which to touch the world, my "*Vollmachtsbrief zum Glücke*": was I to give it unused back to God? I could sing: not that only; I could compose music,—the highest soul-utterance. I remember clutching my hands up to my throat, as if holding safe the power that should release me, suffer me to grow again, and looking across the oil-lamp on the table at my husband. I *had* been called, then,—set apart to a mission; it was a true atom of the creative power that had fired my brain; my birth had placed me on a fitting plane of self-development, and I had thrust it all aside—for what? A mess of weakest pottage,—a little love, silly rides behind Tinker, petting and paltering such as other women's souls grew imbecile without. It was the consciousness of this that had grown slowly on me in the year just gone; I had put my husband from me day by day because of it; it had reached its intolerable climax to-night. Well, it was fact: no fancy. My nature was differently built from others: I could look now at my husband, and see the naked truth about us both. Two middle-aged people, with inharmonious intellects; tastes and habits jarring at every step, clenched together only by faith in a vague whim or fever of the blood called love. Better apart: we were too old for fevers. If I remained with Doctor Manning, my *role* was outlined plain to the end: years of cooking, stitching, scraping together of cents: it was the fate of thousands of married women without means, to grovel every year nearer the animal life, to grow niggardly and common. Better apart.

As I thought that, he laid Teddy down, and came towards me,—the usual uncertain, anxious half-smile on his face with which he regarded me.

"I am sure they will all like my old home, now, lads

and all. I'm glad of that. Sure of all but you, Hester. But you say nothing."

"The loss is great."

I shut my lips firmly, and leaned back, for he had put his hard hand gently on my shoulder. It made me turn faint, with some weakness that must have come down to me from my infant days, so meaningless was it. I did not hear his answer; for with the same passionate feebleness I caught the sleeve of his dressing-gown in my fingers, and began smoothing it. It was the first thing I had ever made for him. I remembered how proud I was the evening he put it on. He was looking down steadily at me with his grave, reasonable eyes, and speaking when I looked up.

"I have been knocked up and down so perpetually in my own life: that may be the reason the change did not trouble me as it ought. It makes one feel as if outside matters were but just the tithes of mint and cumin,—a hurly-burly like that which I've lived in. I am sorry. I thought you would grieve least of all, Hester. You are stronger-brained than we Mannings, eh? I was sure the life meant so much more to you than food or raiment."

"What do you mean by the life? Have I found it here, Daniel?"

"No, Hester?"

"I want work fit for me," I said almost fiercely. "God made me for a good, high purpose."

"I know," cheerfully: "We'll find it, dear: no man's work is kept back from him. We'll find it together."

But under the cheerfulness there was a sad quiet, as

of one who has lost something forever, and tries to hide the loss from himself. There was a moment's silence, then I got up, and pushed him down into my chair. I took the gray head in my arms, leaned it on my shoulder, held the thin bits of hair in my hand.

"Why, why, child!"

"Call me Hetty, Daniel. I'd like to think that name belonged to me yet."

"Surely, dear. Why! but—this is just the old times again, Hetty! You'll be bringing me my slippers again."

"Yes, I will."

I went to the cupboard, and brought them, sitting down on the floor as he put them on. Another of the old foolish tricks gone long ago. There was a look on his face which had not been there this many a day. He had such a credulous heart, so easy to waken into happiness. I took his wrist in my bony hands, to raise myself; the muscles were like steel, the cording veins throbbing with health; there was an indescribable rest in the touch.

"Daniel," I said, looking him full in the face, "I'd like to have no mission in God's world. I'd like to give up my soul, and forget everything but you."

He did not answer. I think now that he understood me then and before far better than I dreamed. He only put his hand on mine with an unutterable tenderness. I could read nothing on his face but a grave common-sense. Presently he unbuttoned my sleeves and the close collar about my throat to let the cool damp blow on me.

"Yes," I said, "it's a fever, Daniel. In the blood. That is all,—with me. I decided that long ago. It will not last long." And I laughed.

"Come," he said quietly. "I am going to write Rob now, about our plans. You can help me."

I followed him, and sat down by the table. "There is something in the man stronger than the woman," I thought, doggedly, "inside of blood and muscle." Yet the very galling of that consciousness set me more firmly in the mind to be again free.

A month after that we came to Newport. It was not an idle month. Jacky had proposed a review of my husband's and his sons' clothes, and day after day I had sat by the window looking out on the sluggish Hudson, a hank of patent thread about my neck, stitching patches on the stiff, half-worn trousers. "It becomes us to take care of the pence now," she would say, and go on with her everlasting whistling. La-la. It rasped on my brain like the chirp of the partridge outside in the cedar-hedge. When she would go out of the room sometimes, I would hold my hand to my head, and wonder if it was for this in reality God had made me.

Yet I had my own secret. The work of my life, before I was married, had been the score of an opera. I got it out now by stealth, at night, putting my pen to it here and there, with the controlled fever with which a man might lay his hand on a dear dead face, if he knew the touch would bring it back to life. Was there any waking that dead life of mine? At that time, in New York, M. Vaux was trying the experiment of an English opera in one of the minor theatres. I sent the score to him. It did not trouble me, that, if produced, its first effect would be tried on an uncultured caste of hearers: if the leaven was pure, what matter where it began to work? and no poet or artist was ever more sincere in the belief that the divine power spoke through him than I. I thought, that, if I remained with Doctor Manning as his wife, this venture mattered little: if I shook myself free, and, taking up my mission, came before the public as a singer, it would open the way for me. For my plan had grown defined and practical to me now.

M. Vaux had left his family at Newport after the season was over. I was to meet him there when we went down, and hear his decision on the score. I met him one day on Broadway, and hinted my vague desire of making my voice also available.

"To sing? did you say sing, Mrs. Manning? go on the stage?"—pawing his chin with one hand.

He was a short, puffy little man, with a bullet head at half-cock in the air, producing a general effect of nostrils on you.

"Sing, eh?" he mumbled, once or twice.

Before this I had been Mrs. Manning, throwing off an opera-score as a careless whim, one of the class to whom he and his like presented arms: he surveyed me now with the eye of a stock-raiser buying a new mule, and set the next evening as the time when I should "drop in at his house and give him a trill or two. — Keeping dark before the old man yet, eh?" with a wink. I went in the next day, but he declined to pronounce judgment until we came to Newport.

I remember my husband met me at the gate when I returned, and lifted me from the little pony-carriage.

"I'm so glad my girl is taking her drives again."—his face in a glow,—"coming back with the old red cheeks, too. They're a sort of hint of all the good years coming. We're far off from being old people yet, Hetty." And so went beside me slowly up the garden-walk, his hands clasped behind him, stopping to look now and then at his favorite purple and crimson hollyhocks.

I looked at him askance, as we went through the evening shadows. There was something grand in the quiet of the face, growing old with the depth of sadness and endurance subdued in it: the kindly smile over all. I had brought the smile there. But it would not be for long: and I remember how the stalk of gillyflower I held snapped in my hand, and its spicy odor made me throw it down. I have loathed it ever since. Was my life to be wasted in calling a smile to an old man's face? My husband and M. Vaux were different men; but, on the other side, they were gates to me of different lives: here, a sordid slavery of work; there,—something in me glowed warm and triumphant,—fame and an accomplished deed in life!

Surely these mawkish home-ties were fast loosing their hold on me, I thought, as we went in. I asked no questions as to my husband's plans; no one spoke to me of them. In the few days before our departure I roped up chairs, packed china in straw, sorted clothes into trunks, working harder than the others, and then creeping off alone would hum an air from the score, thanking God for giving me this thoroughly pure, holy message to utter in the world. It was the redemption of my soul from these vulgar taints: it was a sort of mortgage I held on the eternal truth and life. Yet, when no one told me of their plans, when I saw they all held some secret back from me, watching me constantly and furtively, when Jacky buzzed about my husband all day, whispering, laughing, cooking his favorite omelet for breakfast, bringing his slippers at night,—it was like so many sharp stings through stupor. "It's the woman's flesh of me!" I used to say bitterly, when I would have been glad to meanly creep after them, to cuddle Teddy up in my arms, or to lean my head on his father's knees. "I can live it down. I have 'a manly soul.'" For it was part of my creed that Nature was something given us to be lived down in fulfilling our mission.

We went by the evening's boat to Newport. I saw M. Vaux in the outer cabin, as we passed through: he nodded familiarly when Doctor Manning's back was turned, without removing his cigar.

It was stifling below, with the smell of frying meat and numerous breaths. We went on deck, my husband drawing a bench around to shelter me from the keen wind across the bow, and wrapping my flannel hood closer to my throat when we drifted out within scent of salt water. It was a night that waited and listened: the sea silent and threatening, a few yellow, dogged, low breakers running in at long intervals; now and then a rasping gurgle of wind from shore, as of one who held his breath; some thin, brown clouds ragged along the edges of the cold sky, ready for flight.

I sat there thinking how well the meaning of the sea suited my soul that night. It was no work of God's praising Him continually: it was the eternal protest and outcry against Fate,—chained, helpless, unappealing. Let the mountains and the sunshine and the green fields chant an anthem, if they would; but for this solitary sea, with its inarticulate cry, surely all the pain and impatience of the world's six thousand years had gone down and found a voice in that. Having thus cleared to myself the significance of the sea in Nature, I was trying to define its exact effect upon my own temperament, (a favorite mental exercise of my father's,) when my husband touched my shoulder.

"I'll go down and smoke a bit, Hetty dear, and leave you with Jacky. She's as good guard as a troop of horse."

Jacky nodded vehemently once or twice from where she stood, followed him with her eyes as he went down the steps, anxiously, and then stood gravely silent. She was but a lump of "woman's flesh," that was clear, and I doubted if there was any soul inside to live it down. Her face was red and her eyes shining with the sea-wind. She had been at the stern with the boys, making a riot about the porpoises rolling under the boat; in the engine-room with Teddy; had tried to drag me to the deck-railing to watch the unsteady shimmer of some pale-blue sea-weed under the water, which the wheel threw up in silver flashes, and to see how, before the sun went down, we floated over almost motionless stretches of pale tea-colored water, holding, it seemed, little curdling pools of light far below in their depths on depths of shivering brown and dull red mosses.

"Ach-h! I'm glad I'm alive tonight!" she had said, gritting her teeth in her Dutch fashion.

But some new demon had possession of her brain now: she stood working with her shawl uncertainly, a trifle pale, watching me. She came to me at last, and stood balancing herself first on her heels and then her toes, biting her lip as if doubtful how to begin.

"I wish we had the baby along!" came with a gruff burst, finally. "God bless its little soul! I went out to see it on Saturday. It would do Uncle Daniel good. He needs something fresh and hearty, bread-and-butter-like, or a baby. You did not notice him this evening particularly, Mrs. Manning, eh?" anxiously.

"No."

"Nothing—Well, no matter. I'm fanciful, maybe. There's an old saying in the family about him, some Doctor's prophecy, and it makes me over-watchful, likely."

She waited for a question. I asked none. There was a dull throb of pain in my heart, but I thrust it down. The girl waited a few moments, debating with herself: I could read the struggle on her face: then she looked up straight into my eyes, her small white teeth showing determined as a steel-trap.

"It's quiet here, Mrs. Manning, and will be for a bit, and there's a story I'd like to tell you. It would do me good, if it were off my mind. Perhaps you, too," with a sharp glance.

"Go on."

She put her hand into her pocket and pulled out a broken morocco case.

"Look here. This tells the whole of the story, almost,"—holding it where the light from the cabin-window fell on it.

It was the daguerreotype of a woman: one of those faces that grow out of a torpid, cunning, sensual life; apparently marked, too, by some strange disease, the skin white, and hanging loose from the flesh. I pushed it away. Jacqueline polished it with her palm.

"She was an opium-eater, you see? The eyes have that rigid staring, like Death looking into life. You pushed it from you, Mrs. Manning?"—shutting it. "Yet I know a man who cherished that living face tenderly in his bosom for fifteen long years, and never opened his lips to say to God once that it was hard to bear: faugh!" and she flung the case into the water. "I only kept it to show you. She, the foul vampire, sucked his youth away. I think it was but the husk of a life that was left him when she died;—and we are making that mean and poor enough,"—in a lower voice. "Yet that man"—more firmly—"has a stronger brain and fresher heart than you or I are fit to comprehend, Mrs. Manning. One would think God meant that the last of his life, after that gone, should be a warm Indian-summer day, opening broad and happily into the life He is keeping for him,—would you not?"

"Who is the man?"—my lips growing cold.

"Your husband."

"I thought so. You did well to tell me that story."

She looked from me, her color coming and going.

"It was hard to do it. You are an older woman than I. But I thought it was needed."

I looked up at the hard-set, chubby little face, beyond at the far yellow nightline of the sea, listened to the low choke, choke, of the water in the wheels.

"I wish you would leave me. Let me be alone awhile."

She went to the other end of the deck, where she could keep me in sight. It was so dull, that throb of the water, playing some old tune that would not vary! The sea stretched out in such blank, featureless reaches!

To nestle down into this man's heart and life! To make his last years that warm Indian-summer day! I could do it! I! What utter rest there were in that!

Yet was this power within me to rot and waste? My nature, all the habit and teaching of the years gone, dragged me back, held up my Self before me, bade me look at that. A whiff of tobacco-scented breathing made me look up. M. Vaux was leaning on the deck-railing, his legs crossed, surveying me critically through his half-shut eyes.

"Well, 'm glad of the chance t' tell you. Henz and Doctor Howe thought so well of that little thing of yours that we've put it in rehearsal,—bring it out Monday week. 'N' 've concluded you can try the part of Marian in it. Not much in that,—one aria you can make something of, but begin easy, hey?"

"I have concluded to give up that scheme, Monsieur."

"Tut! tut! No such thing. Why, you've a master-talent,—that is, with cultivation, cultivation. A fine gift, Madam. Belongs to the public. Why," tapping his yellow teeth with his cane-head, "it's shutting up a bird in a cage, to smother a voice like yours. Must have training,—yes, yes, 'll see to that; 'n' there are tricks and bits of stage-effect; but you'll catch 'em,—soon enough. There's other little matters," with a furtive glance at my square shoulders and bony figure, "necessary to success. But you'll understand."

I saw how anxious the man was that I should accede to the proposal. I had not overrated my genius, then?

"If the thing's to be done, let it be done quickly. I'm going to run back to town to-morrow night, and you'd best go with me, and can go in rehearsal at once. You can break it to your people to-morrow. I'll meet you in the boat,—that is," with an unwilling hesitation, "if you decide to go."

Jacky approached us.

"I will let you know," I said; and as he walked away, the water began its dull throb, again, that lasted all night long.

All night long! Other people may approach the crisis of their fate with senses and faculties all on guard and alert; but with me, although I knew the next day would witness my choice for life, I believe that heavy thud of water was the most real thought, trying my brain beyond endurance. I tried to reason coolly in the night about M. Vaux and his scheme: both vulgar, degrading in outside appearance,—I felt that, to the quick, keenly enough; but inside lay a career, utterance for myself,—and I had been dumb and choking so long!

A beam of light from the cabin-chandelier struck just then sharply across Doctor Manning's face, where he lay asleep in his berth. There was an unusual look in it, as Jacky had said, now that I looked closely: a blueness about the mouth, and a contraction of the nostrils. Was it a hint of any secret disease, that she had looked so terrified, and even the boys had kept such a sidelong scrutiny over him all day? I sat up. If I could go to him, put my hands about his head, cling to him, let my young strength and life ooze into his to atone for all he had lost in those old days! There was passion and power of love under my stiff-muscled fingers and hard calculating brain, such as these people with their hot blood knew nothing of. It was passion, a weak fever of the flesh. I drew the sheet over me, and lay down again.

The morning was stiflingly hot. I remember the crowd of porters, drays, etc., jostling on the wharf: the narrow street: Monsieur passing me, as we turned into it, and muttering, "By six this afternoon I must know your decision": Robert's grave, inquiring face, when he first met his father, and saw his changed look. The rooms he had taken for us were but partially furnished, carpetless, the sun staring in through dirty windows, blue and yellow paper on the walls. He went out with Dr. Manning for a walk; the boys scattered off noisily to the sea-side. I went to work making a sort of lounge for Teddy to sleep on, out of some blocks of wood and staves of an old barrel, and so passed the time until noon. Then I sat down to mend the weekly heap of boys' socks, half-washed and leather-stained. Out of the window where I sat I looked down into the muddy back-yard of the boarding-house, where an Irishwoman was washing and gossiping with the cook cleaning fish over the ash-heap. *This* was what Life held for me now, was it? When the door was opened, a strong whiff of dinner filled the room. Two o'clock came.

"I will not go down to dinner," I said to Jacqueline, when the cracked bell rang. "I will go out and find Doctor Manning on the cliffs. I may have something to say to him."

But when she was gone, I darned on at the unclean socks. Somehow the future faced me in my work and surroundings. But I did not think of it as a whole. The actual dignity and beauty of life, God's truth itself, may have grown dim to me, behind a faint body and tired fingers; but let the hard-worked woman who is without that sin throw the first stone at me. I got up at last, folded the stockings, and put them away; then pinned on my bonnet and shawl. Teddy was sitting on the stairs, half asleep. I stopped to kiss him.

"You'll be back soon, mother?"—hugging me close about the neck.

"Good bye, Bud! Bring your father his pipe to-night, as he likes you to do,—and every night."

I strained him close to my breast again; he had a warm, honest little heart of his own; he would be such a man as his father. I gasped, set him down: I dared not kiss him after I thought of that: and went out of the hall, stumbling over the boarders' hats and greasy oil-cloth. Without, the air had that yellow stirless calm peculiar to Newport, which gives to the sea and landscape the effect of those French pictures glassed in tinted crystal. There were but few passengers on the street. I wondered if any of them held his fate in his hand as I did mine that day. Before I reached the cliffs the afternoon was passing away rapidly; the heated pavements under my feet growing cooler, and barred with long gray shadows; a sea-breeze blowing tattered sand-colored clouds inland; the bell of the steamer rang out sharply down at the quiet little wharf. In half an hour she would sail. M. Vaux was on board, awaiting me. I had but little time to spare.

I turned and crept slowly along the road to where the grassy street opened on the cliffs, and sat down on the brown rocks. I could see my husband on the sands with Robert, pacing to and fro; the scent of their cigars almost reached me where I sat. I must see him once more. The bell of the boat rang again; but I sat still, breaking off bits of the salt crust from the rock, hardly looking up to see if her steam was up. I was going. I knew she would not sail until I was on board. And I must see him again; he would call me Hetty, maybe: that would be something to remember. It was very quiet. The bare, ghastly cliffs formed a sort of crescent, on which I sat; far below, the sea rolled in, over the white sand, in heavy ashen sweeps: in one horn of the crescent the quaint old town nestled, its smoky breath sleepily giving good-night to the clear pink air; in the other stood the sullen fort, the flag flapping sharply against the sky. The picture cut itself vividly on my brain. The two black figures came slowly towards me, across the sands, seeing me at last. I would not tell him I was going: I could write from New York: I thought, my courage giving way. What a hard, just face Robert Manning had! What money I made should go to the support of my child: Robert should not think me derelict in every duty. Then I tried to get up to meet them, but leaned back more heavily on the rocks, twisting my fingers in a tuft of salt hay that grew there.

I heard Robert say something about "jaded" and "overworked," as he looked at me, throwing away his cigar; his father answered in a whisper, which made the young man's face soften, and when they came near, he called me "mother," for the first time. Into the face of the man beside him I did not look: I thought I never could look again. There was a small rip in the sleeve of his great-coat: I remember I saw it, and wondered feebly if Jacky would attend to it,—if my child, when she was a woman, would be careful and tender with her father. Meantime my husband was talking in his cheerfullest, heartiest voice.

"Coming here makes me feel as if the old boy-time had come back, Hetty. Rob and I have been planning out our new life, and the sea and the fresh air and the very houses seemed to join in the talk, and help me on as they used to do then. I'll begin all new; just as then. Only now"—

He put his hand on my shawl with a motion that had

infinite meaning and affection in it. The little steamer at the wharf swayed and rocked. Her freight was nearly all on deck: I had but a few moments more,—that is, if I meant to be free.

"We are going down to the hotel for a few minutes,—business, Hetty," he said. "Will you wait for us here? or are you afraid to be alone?"

"No, I'm not afraid to be alone. It is better for me."

"Good bye, then. Come, Rob."

I did not say good-bye. Even then, I think I did not know what I had resolved. I thrust my fingers deeper into the wet tuft of grass, heard the long dash of the breakers on the beach, looked at the square black figure of Robert Manning as it went slowly up the sandy road into the street. At the other, taller and more bent, beside it, I did not once look. I wiped the clammy moisture off my face and throat.

"It's the woman's flesh of me," I said. "There is better stuff in me than that. I will go now, and fulfill my calling."

On the wharf, as I went creeping along, I met Monsieur. He offered me his fat little arm, with smiles and congratulations, and handed me hurriedly over the plank on to the deck. In a moment the steamer was puffing out of harbor.

I was to play Marian in my own opera. God had given me a power of headwork, skill for a certain mission, and I was going to perform it. The vast, vague substance on which I was to act was brought before me to-night, palpable,—the world, posterity, time; how did I call it? But, somehow, it was not what I had dreamed of since my babyhood up yonder in Concord. Nothing was vast or vague. I was looking into a little glass in a black-painted frame, and saw the same Mrs. Manning, with the same high cheekbones, the yellow mole on the upper lip, the sorrowful brown eyes: dressed in tulle now, though, the angular arms and shoulders bare, and coated with chalk, a pat of rouge laid on each cheek: under the tulle-body the same old half-sickness; the same throbbing back-tooth threatening to ache. The room was small, triangular: a striped, reddish cotton carpet on the floor, a door with a brass handle, my bandbox open on a chair, a basin with soapy water, soiled towels, two dripping tallow-candles: in short, a dressing-room in a theatre. Outside, wheels, pulleys, pasteboard castles, trees, chairs, more bony women, more chalk, more tulle. Monsieur in a greasy green dressing-gown odorous of tobacco, swearing at a boy with blear eyes,—a scene-shifter. The orchestra tuning beyond the footlights: how vilely the first violin slurred over that second passage! "Life's Prophecy," I called it; and that "Vision of Heaven," the trombonist came in always false on the bass, because, as Monsieur said, he had always two brandy-slings too much. Beyond was "the world," passive, to be acted upon; the parquet,—ranged seats of young men with the flash-stamp on them from their thick noses to the broad-checked trousers; the dress-circle,—young girls with their eyes and brains full-facing their attendant sweethearts, and a side-giggle for the stage; crude faces in the gallery, tamed faces lower down; gray and red and black and tow-colored heads full of myriad teeming thoughts of business, work, pleasure, outside of this: treble and tenor notes wandering through them, dying almost ere born; touching what soul behind the dress and brain-work? and touching it how? Ah, well! "I am going to fulfil my mission." I said that, again and again, as I stood waiting. "Now. This is it. I take it up." But my blood would not be made to thrill.

"This wart must be covered," said a walking-lady in red paper-muslin, touching the mole on my lip with Meen Fun. M. Vaux tapped at the door,—a sly, oily smile on his mouth.

"We are honored to-night. Be prepared, my dear Madam, for surprises in your audience. Your husband is in the house,—and his son, Robert Manning."

I put up my hands in the vain effort to cover the bare neck and shoulders,—then, going back into the dressing-room, sat down, without a word. I remember how the two tallow-candles flared and sputtered, as I sat staring at them; how on the other side of the brass-handled door the play went on, the pulleys creaked, and the trombones grated, and the other women in tulle and chalk capered and sang, and that at last the stuffy voice of the call-boy outside cried, "Marian, on," and it was my time to fulfil my mission. I remember how broad a gap the green floor of the stage made to the shining tin foot-lights; how the thousand brassy, mocking eyes were centred on the lean figure that moved forward; how I heard a weak quaver going up, and knew it to be my own voice: I remember nothing more until the scene was ended: the test and last scene of the opera it had been: and as the curtain fell, it was stopped by a faint, dismal hiss that grew slowly louder and more venomous, was mingled with laughs and jeers from the gallery, and the play was damned. I stood with my white gauze and bony body and rouge behind a pasteboard flower-vase, and looked out at the laughing mob of faces. This was the world; I had done my best headwork for it, and even these plebeian brains had found it unfit for use, and tossed it aside. I waited there for a moment, and then passing Monsieur, whose puffy face was purple with disappointment and rage, went into the dressing-room.

"What wonder?" I heard him demand in French. "It was so coarse a theft! But I hoped the catch-dresses would pass it off."

I wrapped a flannel cloak over my airy robes, and went out, down the crooked back-stairs into the street. I had no money; if I went back to the hotel where I had been stopping, it would be as a beggar.

I waited outside of the theatre by an old woman's candy-stand for the crowd to hustle past, holding myself up by her chair-back. She was nodding, for it was past midnight, but opened her red eyes to lift a little child on her knees who had been asleep at her feet.

"Come, Puss, the play's out, it's time for you an' Granny to be snug at home."

I laughed. Why, there was not one of these women

or men crowding by, the very black beggar holding your horse, who had not a home, a child to touch, to love them,—not one. And I—I had my Self. I had developed that.

I pulled the cloak closer about me and went down the pavement. The street was thronged with street-cars stopping for the play-goers, hacks, and omnibuses; the gas flamed in red and green letters over the house-fronts; the crowd laughed and swayed and hummed snatches of songs, as they went by. I saw one or two husbands drawing the wrappings tighter about their wives' throats, for the air was sharp. My husband had seen my shoulders to-night,—so had they all, covered with chalk. There were children, too, cuddling close to their mothers' sides in the carriages. I wondered if my child would ever know it had a mother. So I went slowly down the street. I never saw the sky so dark and steeling a blue as it was that night: if there had been one star in it, I think it would have looked softer, more pitying, somehow, when I looked up. Knowing all that I had done, I yet cannot but feel a pity for the wretch I was that night. If the home I had desolated, the man and child I had abandoned, had chosen their revenge, they could not have asked that the woman's flesh and soul should rise in me with a hunger so mad as this.

At the corner of the street, a group from the crowd had stopped at the door of a drug-shop; they were anxious, curious, whispering back to those behind them. Some woman fainting, perhaps, or some one ill. I could not pass the lock of carriages at the crossing, and stopped, looking into the green light of the window-bottles. In a moment I caught my own name, "Manning," from a policeman who came out, and a word or two added. The crowd drew back with a sudden breath of horror; but I passed them, and went in. It was a large shop: the lustres, marble soda-fountains, and glittering shelves of bottles dazzled me at first, but I saw presently two or three men, from whom the crowd had shrunk away, standing at the far end of the shop. Something lay on the counter among them,—a large, black figure, the arm hanging down, the feet crossed. It did not move. I do not know how long I stood there, it might be hours, or minutes, and it did not move. But I knew, the first moment I looked at it, that it would never move again. They worked with him, the three men, not speaking a word. The waistcoat and shirt were open; there was a single drop of blood on the neck, where they had tried to open a vein. After a while the physician drew back, and put his hand gently on the shoulder of the shorter, stouter of the other two men,

"My friend," he said, compassionately.

Robert Manning did not seem to hear him. He had knelt on the floor and hid his face in the hand that hung down still and cold. The druggist, a pale, little person, drew the doctor aside.

"What is it, now? Apoplexy?" his face full of pity.

"No. Brought on by nervous excitement,—heart, you know. Threatened a long time, his son says. His wife, the woman who"—

The policeman had been eying my dress under the cloak for some time.

"Hi! *You*'d best move on," he whispered. "This a'n't no place for the likes of you."

I stood still a moment, looking at the brawny black figure lying on the counter. The old days of Tinder and the paddock,—I don't know why I thought of them. It did not move: it never would move again. Dead. I had murdered him. I! I got my fingers in my oily hair, and pulled at it. "Hetty, Hetty Manning," I said, "good bye! Good bye, Daniel!" I remember hearing myself laugh as I left the shop-door; then I went down the street.

When I was far down the Bowery, an old thought came feebly up in my brain. It was how the water had choked, choked, all that night long in the wheel of the boat. When I thought of that, I waited to think. Then I turned and went to the bay, beyond Castle Garden.

The rain, drip, dripping on a cottage-roof: on branches, too, near at hand, that rustled and struck now and then against the little window-shutters, in a fashion just dreary enough to make one nestle closer into the warm bed, and peep out into the shadowy chamber, with the cozy little fire burning hotly in the grate. Patter, patter: gurgling down the spouts: slacking for a minute, threatening to stop and let you sleep in a usual, soundless, vulgar way, as on other nights; then at it again, drip, drip, more monotonous, cheerfuller in its dreariness than ever. Thunder, too: growling off in the hills, where the night and rain found no snug little bed-room to make brighter by their besieging: greenish-white jets of lightning in the cracks of the shutters, making the night-lamp on the toilet-table and the fire suddenly go out and kindle up fiercely again.

This for a long time: hours or not, why should one try to know? A little bed, with crimson curtains, cool white pillows: a soft bed, where the aching limbs rested afresh with every turn. After a while, a comfortable, dumpling little figure in a loose wrapper, popping out of some great chair's depths by the fire and stirring some posset on the hearth: smelling at a medicine-bottle: coming to the bed-side, putting a fat hand on one's forehead: a start, a nervous kiss, a shaky little laugh or two, as she fumbles about, saying, "Hush-h!" and a sudden disappearing behind the curtains. A grave, pale face looking steadily down, as if afraid to believe, until the dear eyes fill with tears, and the head, with its old wig, is dropped, and I and God only know what his soul is saying.

"My husband!"

"Hetty!"

"Is it you?—Daniel?"

He lifted me in his arms farther up on the pillow, smoothing the blankets about me, trying to speak, but only choking, in a ridiculous fashion.

"And the opera, and the drug-shop, and"—

I held my hand to my head.

"The truth is," said Jacky, bobbing out from behind the curtains, her eyes suspiciously red and shiny, "I'm afraid you've had some bad dreams, dear. Just take a teaspoonful of this, that's a good soul! You've been ill, you see. Brain-fever, and what not. The very day we came to Newport. Uncle Daniel and Robert found you on the cliff."

"When we came from the hotel, you remember?" still pulling the blanket up, his lip unsteady.

"You'll choke her; what a nurse you are, to be sure, Uncle Dan! And the woman's feet as bare"—

"There, there, Jacky! I know,"—submissively, twitching at my nightcap, and then gathering my head into his arms until I could hear how his heart throbbed under the strong chest. "My wife! Hetty! Hetty!" he whispered.

I knew he was thanking God for giving me to him again. *I* dared not think of God, or him: God, that had given me another chance.

I lay there until morning, weak and limp, on his arm, touching it now and then to be sure it was alive, an actual flesh-and-blood arm,—that I was not a murderer. Weak as any baby: and it seemed to me—it comes to me yet as a great truth—that God had let me be born again: that He, who gave a new life to the thief in his last foul breath, had given me, too, another chance to try again. Jacky, who was the most arbitrary of nurses, coiled herself up on the foot of the bed, and kept her unwinking eyes sharp on us to enforce silence. Never were eyes more healthful and friendly, I thought, feebly. But I tried all the time to press my poor head in closer to my husband's breast: I was barely free from that vacuum of death and crime, and in there were the strength and life that were to save me; I knew that.

God, who had brought me to this, alone knew how I received it: whether it was a true wife that lay on Daniel Manning's bosom that night; how I loathed the self I had worshipped so long; how the misused, diseased body and soul were alive with love for him, craved a week's, a day's life to give themselves utterly to him, to creep closer to him and the Father that he knew so simply and so well. I heard him once in the night, when he thought I was asleep, say to himself something of the wife who had been restored to him, who "was dead and is alive again, was lost and is found." But how true those words were he can never know.

I fell asleep towards morning, and when I woke, it was with a clear head and stronger eye to comprehend my new chance in life. The room had a pure, fresh, day-light look, snug and tidy; a clear fire crackled on the clean hearth; Jacky herself had her most invigorating of morning faces, going off at the least hint of a joke into redness and smiles. It rained still, but the curtains were drawn back, and I could see through the gray wet what a pleasant slope of meadow there was outside, clumped over with horse-chestnuts and sycamores, down to a narrow creek. The water was fogged over now with drifting mist, but beyond I caught glimpses of low wooded hills, and far to the left the pale flush of the sea running in on the sand. My husband was watching me eagerly as I looked out.

"I do not know where I am, Daniel."

"No, of course you don't,"—rubbing his forehead, as he always did when he was especially pleased. "There's so much to tell you, Hetty dear! We're beginning all new again, you see!"

"You'll not tell a word, until she's had her breakfast," said Jacky, dogmatically, coming with her white basin of cool water.

Oh, the remembrance of that plunge of cold on the hot skin, of the towel's smelling of lavender, of the hard-brushed hair, of the dainty little tray, with its smoking cup of fragrant, amber tea, and delicatest slice of crisp toast! Truly, the woman's flesh of me, having been triumphant so long, goes back with infinite relish to that first meal, and the two bright faces bent over me. And then came Teddy, slying to the pillow-side, watching my pale face and thin hands with an awe-struck gaze, and carrying off the tea and toast to finish by the hearth.

"You can't see much for the rain, mother," anxiously. "Not the orchard, nor the stable,—but there *is* a stable, and hay, and eggs every morning, only the gray hen's trying to set, if you'll believe it. And old Mary's in the kitchen, and we've got even Tinder and our old peacock from the Hudson."

"Eat your toast now, Captain," said his father, putting his arm about me again.

"Yes, Hetty, it's a bit of a farm,—ten or fifteen acres. Our cozery: yours and mine, dear. It's Rob's surprise,"— with the awkward laugh a man gives, when, if he were a woman, the tears would come.

"Rob?"

"Yes. He had it ready. I knew it before we left New

York, but we wanted to surprise you. The boys all put in a little. They're good boys. I've hardly deserved it of them,"—pulling at the quilt-fringe. "I've been a glum, unsociable old dog. I might have made their lives cheerfuller. They're going West: Bill and John to Chicago, and Jem to St. Louis: just waiting for you to be better."

"I am sorry."

I was sorry. The thought of their earnest, honest, downright faces came to me now with a new meaning, somehow: I could enter into their life now: it was an eager affection I was ready to give them, that they could not understand: I had wakened up, so thirsty for love, and to love.

"Yes, Rob did it,"—lingering on the name tenderly. "It's a snug home for us: we'll have to rough it outside a little, but we're not old yet, Hetty, eh?" turning up my face. "I have my old school in town again. We have everything we want now, to begin afresh."

I did not answer; nor, through the day, when Jacky and the boys, one after another, would say anxiously, as one does to a sick person, "Is there anything you need, mother?" did I utter a wish. I dared not: I knew all that I had done: and if God never gave me *that* gift again, I never should ask for it. But I saw them watching me more uneasily, and towards evening caught part of Jacky's talk with Doctor Manning.

"I tell you I will. I'll risk the fever," impatiently. "It's that she wants. I can see it in her eyes. Heaven save you, Uncle Dan, you're not a woman!"

And in a moment she brought my baby and laid it in

my breast. It was only when its little hand touched me that I surely knew God had forgiven me.

It ceased raining in the evening: the clouds cleared off, red and heavy. Rob had come up from town, and took his father's place beside me, but he and Jacky brought their chairs close, so we had a quiet evening all together. Their way of talking, of politics or religion or even news, was so healthy and alive, warm-blooded! And I entered into it with so keen a relish! It was such an earnest, heartsome world I had come into, out of myself! Once, when Jacqueline was giving me a drink, she said,—

"I wish you'd tell us what you dreamed in all those days, dear."

Robert glanced at me keenly.

"No, Jacky," he said, his face flushing.

I looked him full in the eyes: from that moment I had a curious reliance and trust in his shrewd, just, kindly nature, and in his religion, a something below that. If I were dying, I should be glad if Robert Manning would pray for me. I should think his prayers would be heard.

"I will not forget what I dreamed, Robert," I said.

"No, mother. I know."

After that, awhile, I was talking to him of the home he had prepared for his father and me.

"I wanted you just to start anew, with Teddy and the baby, here," he said, lightly.

"And Jacky," I added, looking up at the bright, chubby face.

It grew suddenly crimson, then colorless, then the tears came. There was a strange silence.

"Rob," she whispered, hiding her head sheepishly, "Rob says no."

"Yes, Rob says no," putting his hand on her crisp curls. "He wants you. And mother, here, will tell you a woman has no better work in life than the one she has taken up: to make herself a visible Providence to her husband and child."

I kissed Jacky again and again, but I said nothing. He went away just after that. When he shook hands, I held up the baby to be kissed. He played with it a minute, and then put it down.

"God bless the baby," he said, "and its mother," more earnestly.

Then he and Jacky went out and left me alone with my husband and my child.

# ANNE

It was a strange thing, the like of which had never before happened to Anne. In her matter-of-fact, orderly life mysterious impressions were rare. She tried to account for it afterward by remembering that she had fallen asleep out-of-doors. And out-of-doors, where there is the hot sun and the sea and the teeming earth and tireless winds, there are perhaps great forces at work, both good and evil, mighty creatures of God going to and fro, who do not enter into the little wooden or brick boxes in which we cage ourselves. One of these, it may be, had made her its sport for the time.

Anne, when she fell asleep, was sitting in a hammock on a veranda of the house nearest to the water. The wet bright sea-air blew about her. She had some red roses in her hands, and she crushed them up under her cheek to catch the perfume, thinking drowsily that the colors of the roses and cheek were the same. For she had had great beauty ever since she was a baby, and felt it, as she did her blood, from her feet to her head, and triumphed and was happy in it. She had a wonderful voice too. She was silent now, being nearly asleep. But the air was so cold and pure, and the scent of the roses so strong in the sunshine, and she was so alive and throbbing with youth and beauty, that it seemed to her that she was singing so that all the world could hear, and that her voice rose—rose up and up into the very sky.

Was that George whom she saw through her half-shut eyes coming across the lawn? And Theresa with him? She started, with a sharp wrench at her heart.

But what was Theresa to George? Ugly, stupid, and older than he, a woman who had nothing to win him—but money. *She* had not cheeks like rose leaves, nor youth, nor a voice that could sing at heaven's gate. Anne curled herself, smiling, down to sleep again. A soft warm touch fell on her lips.

"George!"

The blood stopped in her veins; she trembled even in her sleep. A hand was laid on her arm.

"Bless grashus, Mrs. Palmer! hyah's dat coal man wants he's money. I's been huntin' you low an' high, an' you a-sleepin' out'n dohs!"

Anne staggered to her feet.

"Mother," called a stout young man from the tan-bark path below, "I must catch this train. Jenny will bring baby over for tea. I wish you would explain the dampers in that kitchen range to her."

The wet air still blew in straight from the hazy sea horizon; the crushed red roses lay on the floor.

But she—

There was a pier-glass in the room beside her. Going up to it, she saw a stout woman of fifty with grizzled hair and a big nose. Her cheeks were yellow.

She began to sing. Nothing came from her mouth but a discordant yawp. She remembered that her voice left her at eighteen, after she had that trouble with her larynx. She put her trembling hand up to her lips.

George had never kissed them. He had married Theresa more than thirty years ago. George Forbes was now a famous author.

Her fingers still lay upon her lips. "I thought that he—" she whispered, with a shudder of shame through all of her stout old body.

But below, underneath that, her soul flamed with rapture. Something within her cried out, "*I* am here—Anne! I am beautiful and young. If this old throat were different, my voice would ring through earth and heaven."

"Mrs. Palmer, de coal man—"

"Yes, I am coming, Jane." She took her account-book from her orderly work-basket and went down to the kitchen.

When she came back she found her daughter Susan at work at the sewing-machine. Mrs. Palmer stopped beside her, a wistful smile on her face. Susan was so young: she would certainly take an interest in this thing which had moved her so deeply. Surely some force outside of nature had been thrust into her life just now, and turned it back to its beginnings!

"I fell asleep out on the porch awhile ago, Susy," she said, "and I dreamed that I was sixteen again. It was very vivid. I cannot even now shake off the impression that I am young and beautiful and in love."

"Ah, yes! poor dear papa!" Susy said, with a sigh, snipping her thread. She wished to say something more, something appropriate and sympathetic, about this ancient love of her parents; but it really seemed a little ridiculous, and besides, she was in a hurry to finish the ruffle. Jasper was coming up for tea.

Mrs. Palmer hesitated, and then went on into her own room. She felt chilled and defeated. She had thought Susy would take an interest, but— Of course she could not explain to her that it was not of her poor dear papa that she had dreamed. After all, was it quite decent in a middle-aged respectable woman to have such a dream? Her sallow jaws reddened as she shut herself in. She had been very foolish to tell Susy about it at all.

Mrs. Nancy Palmer was always uncomfortably in awe of the hard common-sense of her children. They were both Palmers. When James was a baby he had looked up one day from her breast with his calm attentive eyes, and she had quailed before them. "I never shall be as old as he is already," she had thought. But as they grew up they loved their mother dearly. Her passionate devotion to them would have touched hearts of stone, and the Palmers were not at all stony-hearted, but kindly, good-humored folk, like their father.

The neighborhood respected Mrs. Palmer as a woman of masculine intellect because, after her husband's death, she had managed the plantation with remarkable energy and success. She had followed his exact, methodical habits in peach-growing and in the management of house, had cleared the property of debt, and then had invested in Western lands so shrewdly as to make herself and the children rich.

But James and Susan were always secretly amused at the deference paid to their mother by the good Delaware planters. She was the dearest woman in the world, but as to a business head—

All her peach crops, her Dakota speculations, and the bank stock which was the solid fruit thereof went for nothing as proofs to them of adult good sense. They were only dear mamma's lucky hits. How could a woman have a practical head who grew so bored with the pleasant church sociables, and refused absolutely to go to the delightful Literary Circle? who would listen to a hand-organ with tears in her eyes, and who had once actually gone all the way up to Philadelphia to hear an Italian stroller named Salvini?

Neither of them could understand such childish outbreaks. Give a Palmer a good peach farm, a comfortable house, and half a dozen servants to worry him, and his lines of life were full. Why should their mother be uneasy inside of these lines?

That she was uneasy to-day, Susy soon perceived. A letter came from Pierce and Wall, her consignees in Philadelphia; but Mrs. Palmer threw it down unopened, though she had shipped three hundred crates of Morris Whites last Monday.

She was usually a most careful house-keeper, keeping a sharp eye on the careless negroes, but she disappeared for hours this afternoon, although Jasper Tyrrell was coming for tea, and Jane was sure to make a greasy mess of the terrapin if left to herself.

Jasper certainly had paid marked attention to Susy lately, but she knew that he was a cool, prudent young fellow, who would look at the matter on every side before he committed himself. The Tyrrells were an old, exclusive family, who would exact perfection from a bride coming among them, from her theology to her tea biscuit.

"A trifle of less importance than messy terrapin has often disgusted a man," thought Susy, her blue eyes dim with impatience.

Just before sunset Mrs. Palmer came up the road, her hands full of brilliant maple leaves. Susy hurried to meet and kiss her; for the Palmers were a demonstrative family, who expressed their affection by a perpetual petting and buzzing about each other. The entire household would shudder with anxiety if a draught blew on mamma's neck, and fall into an agony of apprehension if the baby had a cold in its head. Mrs. Palmer, for some reason, found that this habit of incessant watchfulness bored her just now.

"No, my shoes are *not* damp, Susy. No, I did not need a shawl. I am not in my dotage, child, that I cannot walk out without being wrapped up like an Esquimau. One would think I was on the verge of the grave."

"Oh, no, but you are not young, darling mamma. You are just at the age when rheumatisms and lumbagoes and such things set in if one is not careful. Where have you been?"

"I took a walk in the woods."

"Woods! No wonder your shoulders are damp. Come in directly, dear. Four grains of quinine and a hot lemonade going to bed. Walking in the woods! Really, now, that is something I cannot understand,"—smiling at her mother as though she were a very small child indeed. "Now I can walk any distance to church, or to shop, or for any reasonable motive, but to go wandering about in the swampy woods for no earthly purpose—I'll press those leaves for you," checking herself.

"No; I do not like to see pressed leaves and grasses about in vases. It is like making ornaments of hair cut from a dead body. When summer is dead, let it die." She threw down the leaves impatiently, and the wind whirled them away.

"How queer mamma and the people of that generation are—so little self-control!" thought Susy. "It is nearly time for Mr. Tyrrell to be here," she said aloud. "Can Jane season the terrapin?"

"Oh, I suppose so," said Mrs. Palmer, indifferently, taking up a book.

She was indifferent and abstracted all evening. Peter clattered the dishes as he waited at the supper-table, and the tea was lukewarm. Jasper was lukewarm too, silent and critical.

James's wife, Jenny, had come over for supper, and finding her mother-in-law so absent and inattentive, poured forth her anecdotes of baby to Mr. Tyrrell. Jenny, like most young mothers, gave forth inexhaustibly theories concerning the sleep, diet, and digestion of infants. Jasper, bored and uneasy, shuffled in his chair. He had always thought Mrs. Palmer was charming as a hostess, full of tact, in fine rapport with every one. Couldn't she see how this woman was bedevilling him with her croup and her flannels? She was apparently blind and deaf to it all.

Mrs. Palmer's vacant eyes were turned out of the window. Susy glanced at her with indignation. Was mamma deranged?

How petty the pursuits of these children were! thought the older woman, regarding them as from a height. How cautious and finical Tyrrell was in his love-making! Susy too—six months ago she had carefully inquired into Jasper's income.

Tea biscuit and flannels and condensed milk! At seventeen *her* horizon had not been so cramped and shut in. How wide and beautiful the world had been! Nature had known her and talked to her, and in all music there had been a word for her, alone and apart. How true she had been to her friends! how she had hated her enemies! how, when love came to her—Mrs. Palmer felt a sudden chill shiver through her limbs. She sat silent until they rose from table. Then she hurried to her own room. She did not make a light. She told herself that she was absurdly nervous, and bathed her face and wrists in cold water. But she could not strike a light. This creature within her, this Anne, vivid and beautiful and loving, was she to face the glass and see the old yellow-skinned woman?

She ought to think of that old long-ago self as dead.

But it was not dead.

"If I had married the man I loved," this something within her cried, "I should have had my true life. He would have understood me."

How ridiculous and wicked it all was!

"I was a loyal, loving wife to Job Palmer," she told herself, resolutely lighting the lamp and facing the stout figure in the glass with its puffy black silk gown. "My life went down with his into the grave."

But there was a flash in the gray pleading eyes which met her in the glass that gave her the lie.

They were Anne's eyes, and Anne had never been Job Palmer's wife.

Mrs. Palmer did not go down again that night. A wood fire blazed on her hearth, and she put on her wrapper and drew her easy-chair in front of it, with the little table beside her on which lay her Bible and prayer-book and à Kempis. This quiet hour was usually the happiest of the day. James and Jenny always came in to kiss her good-bye, and Susy regularly crept in when the house was quiet to read a chapter with her mother and to tuck her snugly into bed.

But to-night she locked her door. She wanted to be alone. She tried to read, but pushed the books away, and turning out the light, threw herself upon the bed. Not à Kempis nor any holy saint could follow her into the solitudes into which her soul had gone. Could God Himself understand how intolerable this old clumsy body had grown to her?

She remembered that when she had been ill with nervous prostration two years ago she had in an hour suddenly grown eighty years old. Now the blood of sixteen was in her veins. Why should this soul within her thus dash her poor brain from verge to verge of its narrow range of life?

The morbid fancies of the night brought her by

morning to an odd resolution. She would go away. Why should she not go away? She had done her full duty to husband, children, and property. Why should she not begin somewhere else, live out her own life? Why should she not have her chance for the few years left? Music and art and the companionship of thinkers and scholars. Mrs. Palmer's face grew pale as she named these things so long forbidden to her.

It was now dawn. She hastily put on a travelling dress, and placed a few necessary articles and her check-book in a satchel.

"Carry this to the station," she said to Peter, who, half asleep, was making up the fires.

"Gwine to Philadelphy, Mis' Palmer? Does Miss Susy know?"

"No. Tell her I have been suddenly called away."

As she walked to the station she smiled to think how Susy would explain her sudden journey by the letter from Pierce and Wall, and would look to find whether she had taken her overshoes and chamois jacket. "I hate overshoes, and I would like to tear that jacket into bits!" she thought as she took her seat in the car. She was going to escape from it all. She would no longer be happed and dosed and watched like a decrepit old crone. She was an affectionate mother, but it actually did not occur to her that she was leaving Susy and James and the baby. She was possessed with a frenzy of delight in escaping. The train moved. She was free! She could be herself now at last!

It could be easily arranged. She would withdraw her

certificates and government bonds from the vaults of the trust company in Philadelphia. The children had their own property secure.

Where should she go? To Rome? Venice? No. There were so many Americans trotting about Europe. She must be rid of them all. Now there was Egypt and the Nile. Or if another expedition were going to Iceland? Up there in the awful North among the glaciers and geysers, and sagas and Runic relics, one would be in another world, and forget Morris Whites and church sociables and the wiggling village gossip.

"There are people in this country who live in a high pure atmosphere of thought, who never descend to gossip or money-making," she thought, remembering the lofty strains of George Forbes's last poem. "If I had been his wife I too might have thought great thoughts and lived a noble life."

She tried angrily to thrust away this idea. She did not mean to be a traitor to her husband, whom she had loved well and long.

But the passion of her youth maddened her. Job had been a good commonplace man. But this other was a Seer, a Dictator of thought to the world.

The train rolled into Broad Street station. Mrs. Palmer went to the Trust company and withdrew her bonds. She never before had come up to the city alone; Susy always accompanied her to "take care of dear mamma." Susy, who had provincial ideas as to "what people in our position should do," always took her to the most fashionable hotel, and ordered a dinner the cost of which weighed upon her conscience for months afterward. Mrs. Palmer now went to a cheap little café in a back street, and ate a chop with the keen delight of a runaway dog gnawing a stolen bone. A cold rain began to fall, and she was damp and chilled when she returned to the station.

Where should she go? Italy—the Nile—Heavens! there were the Crotons from Dover getting out of the train! She must go somewhere at once to hide herself; afterward she could decide on her course. A queue of people were at the ticket window. She placed herself in line.

"Boston?" said the agent.

She nodded. In five minutes she was seated in a parlor car, and thundering across the bridge above the great abattoir. She looked down on the cattle in their sheds. "I do wonder if Peter will give Rosy her warm mash to-night?" she thought, uneasily.

There were but three seats occupied in the car. Two men and a lady entered together and sat near to Mrs. Palmer, so that she could not but hear their talk, which at first ran upon draughts.

"You might open your window, Corvill," said one of the men, "if Mrs. Ames is not afraid of neuralgia."

Corvill? Ames? Mrs. Palmer half rose from her seat. Why, Corvill was the name of the great figure-painter! She had an etching of his "Hagar." She never looked into that woman's face without a wrench at her heart. All human pain and longing spoke in it as they did in George Forbes's poems. Mrs. Ames, she had heard, was chairman of the Woman's National Society for the Examination of Prisons. Mrs. Palmer had read her exposé of the abominations of the lessee system—words burning with a fiery zeal for humanity. There had been a symposium in Philadelphia, she remembered, of noted authors and artists this week.

No doubt these were two of those famous folk. Mrs. Palmer drew nearer, feeling as if she were creeping up to the base of Mount Olympus. This was what happened when one cut loose from Morris Whites and terrapin and that weary Jane and Peter! The Immortals were outside, and she had come into their company.

"Oh, open the window!" said Mrs. Ames, who had a hoarse voice which came in bass gusts and snorts out of a mouth mustached like a man's. "Let's have some air! The sight of those emigrants huddled in the station nauseated me. Women and babies all skin and bone and rags."

Now Mrs. Palmer had just emptied her purse and almost cried over that wretched group. That sick baby's cry would wring any woman's heart, she thought. Could it be that this great philanthropist had pity only for the misery of the masses? But the man who painted "Hagar" surely would be pitiful and tender?

"Sorry they annoyed you," he was saying. "Some very good subjects among them. I made two sketches," pulling out a note-book. "That half-starved woman near the door—see?—eh? Fine slope in the chin and jaw. I wanted a dying baby for my 'Exiles,' too. I caught the very effect I wanted. Sick child."

Mrs. Palmer turned her revolving chair away. It was a trifling disappointment, but it hurt her. She was in that strained, feverish mood when trifles hurt sharply. These were mere hucksters of art and humanity. They did not belong to the high pure level on which stood great interpreters of the truth—such, for instance, as George Forbes. The little quake which always passed through her at this man's name was increased by a shiver from the damp wind blowing upon her. She sneezed twice.

Mrs. Ames stared at her insolently, and turned her back, fearing that she might be asked to put down the window.

Mr. Corvill was talking about the decoration of the car. "Not bad at all," he said. "There is great tenderness in the color of that ceiling, and just look at the lines of the chairs! They are full of feeling."

Mrs. Palmer listened, bewildered. But now they were looking at the landscape. If he found feeling in the legs of a chair, what new meanings would he not discover in that vast stretch of lonely marsh with the narrow black lagoons creeping across it?

"Nice effect," said Mr. Corvill—"the lichen on that barn against the green. I find little worth using in the fall this year, however. Too much umber in the coloring."

Could it be, she thought, that these people had made a trade of art and humanity until they had lost the perception of their highest meanings?

"I should think," continued Corvill, turning to the

other man, "you could fine *matériel* for some verses in these flats. Ulalume, or The Land of Dolor. Something in that line. Eh, Forbes?"

Forbes! Her breath stopped. That fat hunched man with the greasy black whiskers and gaudy chain! Yes, that was his voice; but had it always that tone of vulgar swagger?

"I've stopped verse-writing," he said. "Poetry's a drug in the market. My infernal publishers shut down on it five years ago."

He turned, and she then saw his face—the thin hard lips, the calculating eye.

Was this man "George"? Or had that George ever lived except in her fancy?

"Mr. Forbes." She rose. The very life in her seemed to stop; her knees shook. But habit is strong. She bowed as she named him, and stood there, smiling, the courteous, thorough-bred old lady whose charm young Tyrrell had recognized. Some power in the pathetic gray eyes startled Forbes and brought him to his feet.

"I think I knew you long ago," she said. "If it is you—?"

"Forbes is my name, ma'am. Lord bless me! you can't be— Something familiar in your eyes. You remind me of Judge Sinclair's daughter Fanny."

"Anne was my name."

"Anne. To be sure. I knew it was Nanny or Fanny. I ought to remember, for I was spoons on you myself for a week or two. You know you were reckoned the best catch in the county, eh? Sit down, ma'am, sit down; people of our weight aren't built for standing."

"Is—your wife with you?"

"You refer to the first Mrs. Forbes—Theresa Stone? I have been married twice since her decease. I am now a widower." He put his hand to his mouth and coughed, glancing at the crape on his hat. His breath crossed her face. It reeked of heavy feeding and night orgies; for Forbes, though avaricious, had gross appetites.

Suddenly Job Palmer stood before her, with his fine clear-cut face and reasonable eyes. He knew little outside of his farm perhaps; but how clean was his soul! How he had loved her!

The car at that moment swayed violently from side to side; the lamps went out. "Hello!" shouted Forbes. "Something wrong! We must get out of this!" rushing to the door. She braced herself against her chair.

In the outside darkness the rushing of steam was heard, and shrieks of women in mortal agony. A huge weight fell on the car, crushing in the roof. Mrs. Palmer was jammed between two beams, but unhurt. A heavy rain was falling.

"I shall not be burned to death, at any rate," she thought, and then fortunately became insensible.

In half an hour she was cut out and laid on the bank, wet and half frozen, but with whole bones. She tried to rise, but could not; every joint ached with rheumatism, her gown was in tatters, the mud was deep under her, and the rain pelted down. She saw the fire burning on her hearth at home, and the easy-chair in front of it, and the Bible and à Kempis.

Some men with lanterns came up and bent over her.

"Great God, mother!" one of them cried. It was James, who had been on the same train, going to New York.

The next day she was safely laid in her own bed. The fire was burning brightly, and Susy was keeping guard that she might sleep. Jenny had just brought a delicious bowl of soup and fed it to her, and baby had climbed up on the bed to hug her, and fallen asleep there. She held him in her arm. James came in on tiptoe, and bent anxiously over her. She saw them all through her half-shut eyes.

"My own—flesh of my flesh!" she thought, and thanked God from her soul for the love that held her warm and safe.

As she dozed, Susy and James bent over her. "Where could she have been going?" said Susy.

"To New York; no doubt to make a better contract than the one she has with Pierce and Wall—to make a few more dollars for us. Or, an investment: her bonds were all in her satchel. Poor dear unselfish soul! Don't worry her with questions, Susy—don't speak of it."

"No, I will not, Jim," said Susy, wiping her eyes. "But if she only had taken her chamois jacket!"

James himself, when his mother was quite well, remarked one day, "We had a famous fellow-traveller in that train to New York—Forbes, the author."

"A most disagreeable, underbred person!" said Mrs. Palmer, vehemently. "I would not have you notice such people, James—a mere shopman of literature!"

\* \* \* \* \* \* \*

Susy married Jasper Tyrrell that winter. They live in the homestead now, and Mrs. Palmer has four or five grandchildren about her, whom she spoils to her heart's content. She still dabbles a little in mining speculations; but since her accident on the cars she is troubled with rheumatism, and leaves the management of the farm and house to Jasper and Susy. She has a quiet, luxurious, happy life, being petted like a baby by all of the Palmers. Yet sometimes in the midst of all this comfort and sunshine a chance note of music or the sound of the restless wind will bring an expression into her eyes which her children do not understand, as if some creature unknown to them looked out of them.

At such times Mrs. Palmer will say to herself, "Poor Anne!" as of somebody whom she once knew that is dead.

*Is* she dead? she feebly wonders; and if she is dead here, will she ever live again?

## More Classic Works from
## the Feminist Press

**But Some of Us Are Brave: Black Women's Studies**
edited by Akasha (Gloria T.) Hull,
Patricia Bell Scott, and Barbara Smith

**Changes: A Love Story** by Ama Ata Aidoo

**Daughter of Earth** by Agnes Smedley

**His Own Where** by June Jordan

**I Love Myself When I Am Laughing . . .
And Then Again When I Am Looking Mean
and Impressive: A Zora Neale Hurston Reader**
edited by Alice Walker

**The Naked Woman** by Armonía Somers,
translated by Kit Maude

**The Native Tongue Trilogy** by Suzette Haden Elgin

**Still Alive: A Holocaust Girlhood Remembered**
by Ruth Kluger

**Thérèse and Isabelle** by Violette Leduc,
translated by Sophie Lewis

**Witches, Midwives & Nurses:
A History of Women Healers**
by Barbara Ehrenreich and Deirdre English

**The Yellow Wall-Paper** by Charlotte Perkins Gilman

**You Can't Get Lost in Cape Town** by Zoë Wicomb

**The Feminist Press** publishes books that ignite movements and social transformation. Celebrating our legacy, we lift up insurgent and marginalized voices from around the world to build a more just future.

See our complete list of books at
**feministpress.org**